Homer

The Wrath of Achilles

Translated by E. V. Rieu
Revised and updated by Peter Jones
with D. C. H. Rieu

PENGUIN ARCHIVE

PENGUIN BOOKS

UK | USA | Canada | Ireland | Australia
India | New Zealand | South Africa

Penguin Books is part of the Penguin Random House group of companies
whose addresses can be found at global.penguinrandomhouse.com

Penguin Random House UK,
One Embassy Gardens, 8 Viaduct Gardens, London SW11 7BW

penguin.co.uk

Penguin
Random House
UK

E. V. Rieu's translation of *The Iliad* first published by Penguin Books 1946
This revised version first published 2003
This extract published in Penguin Classics 2025
003

Revised translation copyright © the Estate of the late E. V. Rieu,
and Peter Jones, 2003
Editorial matter copyright © Peter V. Jones, 2003

Set in 11.2/13.75pt Dante MT Std
Typeset by Jouve (UK), Milton Keynes
Printed and bound in Great Britain by Clays Ltd, Elcograf S.p.A.

The authorized representative in the EEA is Penguin Random House Ireland,
Morrison Chambers, 32 Nassau Street, Dublin D02 YH68

A CIP catalogue record for this book is available from the British Library

ISBN: 978-0-241-74694-3

Penguin Random House is committed to a sustainable future
for our business, our readers and our planet. This book is made from
Forest Stewardship Council® certified paper.

PENGUIN ARCHIVE
The Wrath of Achilles

Homer

c. 700 BCE

A PENGUIN SINCE 1946

Contents

The Main Characters

(The Greeks, and gods affiliated with the Greeks, appear here in roman text, while the Trojans, and gods affiliated with the Trojans, appear in italics.)

GREEKS

ACHILLES [A-kíll-eez]. Son of the mortal Peleus and the divine Sea-nymph THETIS, from Phthia [F-thée-a] in Thessaly [Théss-a-lee]. Leader of the Myrmidons [Mér-midd-ons]. Patroclus is his dearest friend. Achilles' anger drives the story of the *Iliad* [Íll-ee-ad]. ATHENE is always by his side. Homer foretells his death at the hands of *Paris* and *APOLLO*. Called 'swift-footed' because of his speed at chasing down an enemy in flight.

AGAMEMNON [A-ga-mém-non]. Son of Atreus and ruler of Mycenae [My-sée-nee] in Argos. He is leader of the expedition to *Troy* because he brings the most ships. He is the elder brother of Menelaus (the pair are referred to together as the 'sons of Atreus'). He was murdered by his wife Clytaemnestra [Kleye-tem-néss-tra] on his return to Greece.

AJAX, son of Telamon [Áy-jax]. From the island of Salamis [Sáll-a-miss], the 'great' Ajax, defensive bulwark of the Greeks (he never leads an attack), renowned for his huge shield 'like a tower'.

ANTILOCHUS [Ant-íll-ock-us]. Son of Nestor; a young warrior prominent in the fighting and also in the games. Has a brother Thrasymedes [Thrass-imm-éed-eez].

ATREUS [Áy-tr-yoos]. Father of Agamemnon and Menelaus.

AUTOMEDON [Or-to´ m-edd-on]. A Myrmidon, and attendant of Achilles. Serves as attendant and charioteer to Patroclus when he fights without Achilles.

CALCHAS [Kál-kass]. Son of Thestor; the chief augur and prophet of the Greek expedition.

DIOMEDES [Die-om-éed-eez]. Son of Tydeus [Tíe-dyoos] and grandson of Oeneus [Óy-nyoos] – a young but brilliant and much-respected warrior. He is always talking about his father, who was killed in the unsuccessful siege of Thebes ('The Seven against Thebes') and had earlier enjoyed a number of athletic victories there, thanks to ATHENE. A great favourite of ATHENE's.

HELEN. Daughter of ZEUS, sister of Castor and Pollux and Clytaemnestra. Married to Menelaus of Sparta, she caused the Trojan War by running away from him with *Paris* to *Troy*.

MELEAGER [Mell-ee-áy-ger]. A hero cursed by his mother, Althaea [Al-thée-a], for killing her brother in a dispute. He at once withdrew his services from the battlefield – like Achilles.

MENELAUS [Men-ell-áy-us]. Son of Atreus. Ruler
of Lacedaemon/Sparta, and younger brother of
Agamemnon. His wife Helen was seduced and
abducted to *Troy* by *Paris*.

NESTOR [Néss-tor]. Son of Neleus [Née-lyoos].
Ruler of Pylos [Píe-loss]. The oldest of the Greek
chieftains fighting at *Troy*, he has the reputation of
being a fount of wisdom. Called 'Gerenian' [Gerr-
ée-nee-an] – no one knows why.

ODYSSEUS [Odd-íss-yoos]. Son of Laertes [Lay-ért-
ees]. Ruler of Ithaca and hero of Homer's *Odyssey*.
Known for his quick-thinking. A great favourite of
ATHENE's.

PATROCLUS [Pat-róck-lus]. Son of Menoetius. From
Opous; attendant and dearest friend of Achilles.

PELEUS [Péel-yoos]. Father of Achilles, a great warrior
in his day with his horses, armour and famous ash
spear (all given to him by the gods at his wedding to
the Sea-nymph THETIS). Now an old man living
on his own back home in Phthia.

PHOENIX [Fée-nix]. Ruler of the Dolopes and old
friend of Achilles. Peleus made him Achilles'
tutor.

TROJANS AND ALLIES OF *TROY*

AENEAS [Inn-ée-us]. Son of the goddess *APHRODITE*
and mortal *Anchises* [Ank-éye-sees]. Second-in-
command to *Hector*. The hero of Virgil's *Aeneid*, a
Roman epic (19 BCE) about *Aeneas* leaving *Ilium* after

it was sacked by Greeks and founding the Roman race in Italy.

ANDROMACHE [And-ró-mack-ee]. Daughter of *Eëtion*, the ruler of *Thebe* [Thée-bee]. Wife of *Hector* and mother of *Astyanax*.

ASTYANAX [Ast-éye-an-ax]. Son of *Hector* and *Andromache*.

BRISEIS [Briss-áy-iss]. Daughter of *Briseus* from *Lyrnessus*. When Achilles sacked the town, he took *Briseis* captive. Agamemnon subsequently took her from him to compensate himself for the loss of *Chryseis*.

CASSANDRA [Cass-ánd-ra]. Daughter of *Priam* and *Hecabe*. After the sack of *Ilium*, Agamemnon took her home with him, and she was murdered by his wife Clytaemnestra. She was a prophetess who, because she rejected the advances of *APOLLO*, was doomed always to tell the truth and never to be believed.

CHRYSEIS [Cry-sáy-iss]. Daughter of *Chryses* [Crý-seez], the priest of *APOLLO* at *Chryse* [Crý-see] in *Troy*. She was captured at *Thebe* by Achilles and allotted to Agamemnon, who was forced by *APOLLO*'s plague to give her back to her father.

HECABE [Héck-a-bee]. Wife of *Priam*, to whom she bore many sons, including *Hector*, *Paris*, *Helenus* and *Deiphobus*.

HECTOR. Son of *Priam* and *Hecabe*. Married to *Andromache* (with a son *Astyanax*); leader of the *Trojan* and allied armies, and *Troy*'s greatest fighter. Scathing of his elder brother *Paris*.

PARIS. Son of *Priam* and *Hecabe*. Apparently junior to his brother *Hector* (but see under *Hector*). Homer

refers throughout to his abduction of Helen as
the cause of the war but makes only one passing
reference to the famous judgement by *Paris* of
the three goddesses, *APHRODITE*, HERA and
ATHENE, when he was serving as a shepherd on
Mount Ida [Éye-da].

POLYDAMAS [Poll-ídd-a-mus]. Son of *Panthous*. One
of the ablest of the *Trojan* leaders. He is a cautious,
clear-headed strategist whom Homer uses as a
warning figure for *Hector*.

PRIAM [Pr-éye-am]. Son of *Laomedon*, and descendant
of *Dardanus* son of ZEUS (hence 'Dardanian'). Aged
ruler of *Troy*.

SARPEDON [Sar-pée-don]. Son of ZEUS and leader of
the *Trojan* allies from *Lycia*.

GODS

APHRODITE [Aff-rod-éye-tee]. Daughter of ZEUS;
mother of *Aeneas*; lover of the War-god *ARES*; a
goddess primarily associated with sexual impulses.
Since *Paris* selected her as the loveliest of the three
goddesses, she fights on the *Trojan* side. Called
'Cyprian' because of her famous cult-centre on
Cyprus.

APOLLO [A-póll-oh]. Son of ZEUS and *LETO*, also
called *Phoebus*. God of prophecy, sickness and health,
and stringed instruments (hence of the lyre and the
bow). The sudden deaths of men (not by violence) are
attributed to his arrows. He fights on the *Trojan* side.

ARES [Aír-eez]. Son of ZEUS and HERA; the god of war, called 'most hateful' of the gods by ZEUS. He fights on the *Trojan* side, and in the battle of the gods is ignominiously disposed of by ATHENE.

ARTEMIS [Árt-emm-iss]. Daughter of ZEUS and *LETO*, and sister of *APOLLO*; the goddess of hunting and wild animals. She used her arrows to administer a peaceful death for women. On the *Trojan* side.

ATHENE [Ath-ée-nee]. Daughter of ZEUS, also called PALLAS ('Lady'?, 'Mistress'?, 'Youthful'?) ATHENE. Goddess of war, wisdom and the arts and crafts. Strongly pro-Greek because of her defeat in the judgement of *Paris*; works together with HERA against the *Trojans*. 'Grey-eyed' could mean 'owl-eyed', the owl being her special bird. 'Triton-born' may possibly mean that, after ZEUS gave birth to ATHENE from his head, she was then brought up by the River Triton in Greece. 'Atrytone' [A-trý-tonn-ee] remains unexplained.

CRONUS [Crónn-us]. Husband of RHEA [Rée-ah] and father of ZEUS, POSEIDON, HADES and HERA. He was deposed from power by ZEUS, who defeated him in battle and hurled him, with his TITAN supporters, deep underground. He came to power by slicing off his father URANUS' genitals with a sickle (hence ZEUS is 'son of sickle-wielding Cronus').

HADES [Háy-deez]. Son of CRONUS and RHEA. God of the dead, who received the underworld as his portion when he and his brothers ZEUS and

POSEIDON divided the world between them.
Associated with horses.

HEPHAESTUS [Heff-éye-stus]. Son of ZEUS and
HERA. Master craftsman and architect of
Olympus. Pro-Greek. In Homer he was born a
cripple and thrown out of Olympus by ZEUS for
trying to rescue his mother HERA when ZEUS
tied her up.

HERA [Héar-ah]. Daughter of CRONUS and RHEA,
sister and wife of ZEUS. Strongly pro-Greek,
always plotting with ATHENE against ZEUS and
occasionally being punished by him (see under
'Heracles'). Goddess of marriage and motherhood.
'White-armed' perhaps because a fair skin was
valued; 'ox-eyed' perhaps because she was associated
with the cow in prehistoric ritual.

HERMES [Hér-meez]. Son of ZEUS and Maia. The
ambassador of the gods, though in the *Iliad* IRIS
is used more often than HERMES as go-between.
Called 'guide', as he guided the dead down to
HADES; called 'slayer of Argus', a many-eyed
monster sent by HERA to watch over Io, a young
woman ZEUS loved. ZEUS ordered HERMES to
get rid of it.

LETO [Lée-toe]. Mother of *APOLLO* and *ARTEMIS*
by ZEUS.

MUSE. Goddess of memory, who helps the poet sing
about events from long ago.

POSEIDON [Poss-áy-don]. Son of CRONUS and
RHEA, and a younger brother of ZEUS. He

received the sea as his domain when the three brothers, ZEUS, POSEIDON and HADES divided the world by lot between them. God of elemental forces, for example earthquakes. Pro-Greek because he built the walls of *Ilium* for the treacherous *Trojan* ruler *Laomedon*, but received no 'pay' for his work.

THETIS [Thétt-iss]. Daughter of the Old Man of the Sea (Nereus). A Sea-nymph who was married to a mortal, Peleus, father of her only child, Achilles. Always at her son's side when he needs help.

ZEUS [Z-yoos]. Son of CRONUS and RHEA. Sky- and Weather-god (hence 'lord of the lightning flash', 'cloud-gatherer', 'far-thunderer' and so on). Strongest of all the gods and therefore the supreme Olympian deity, the 'Father'. He agrees to support Achilles in his feud with Agamemnon and shows some sympathy for the *Trojans*, in particular *Hector* and *Priam*.

The Wrath of Achilles

Plague and Wrath (Book 1)

The Iliad opens in the tenth year of the war in which the Greeks, led by Agamemnon, have been fighting at Troy. They are trying to win back Helen, wife of Menelaus (Agamemnon's brother), from her Trojan seducer Paris.

The Greeks' greatest fighter, Achilles, has also been attacking, and collecting booty from, Trojan allies in the area, booty which Agamemnon divides up among the army. Agamemnon has recently taken for himself the daughter of the Trojan priest Chryses.

Anger – sing, goddess, the anger of Achilles son of Peleus, that accursed anger, which brought the Greeks endless sufferings and sent the mighty souls of many warriors to Hades, leaving their bodies as carrion for the dogs and a feast for the birds; and Zeus' purpose was fulfilled. It all began when Agamemnon lord of men and godlike Achilles quarrelled and parted.

Which of the gods was it that made them quarrel? It was Apollo, son of Zeus and Leto, who started the feud because he was furious with Agamemnon for not respecting his priest Chryses. So Apollo inflicted a deadly plague on Agamemnon's army and destroyed his men.

Chryses had come to the Greeks' swift ships to recover his captured daughter. He brought with him an immense ransom and carried the emblems of the Archer-god Apollo on a golden staff in his hands. He spoke in supplication to the whole Greek army and most of all its two commanders, Agamemnon and Menelaus, the sons of Atreus:

'Sons of Atreus and you other Greek men-at-arms; you hope to sack Priam's town and get home in safety. May the gods that live on Olympus grant your wish. Now respect the Archer-god Apollo son of Zeus, accept this ransom and release my beloved daughter.'

Then all the other Greeks shouted in agreement. They wanted to see the priest respected and the splendid ransom taken. But this was not at all to Agamemnon's liking. He cruelly and bluntly dismissed the priest:

'Old man, don't let me catch you loitering by the hollow ships today or coming back again in the future, or you may find the god's staff and emblems a very poor defence. That girl I will not release. She will grow old in Argos, in my household, a long way from her country, working at the loom, sharing my bed. Now get out and don't provoke me, if you want to save your skin.'

So he spoke, and the old man was afraid and did as he was told. He went off without a word along the shore of the sounding sea. But when he had gone some distance, the old man poured out prayers to lord Apollo, son of lovely-haired Leto:

'Hear me, Apollo, lord of the silver bow, protector of Chryse and holy Cilla, and mighty ruler over Tenedos! Plague-god, if ever I built a temple that pleased you, if ever I burnt you offerings of the fat thighs of bulls or goats, grant me this wish. Make the Greeks pay with your arrows for my tears.'

So he spoke in prayer, and Phoebus Apollo heard him and came down in fury from the heights of Olympus, his bow and covered quiver on his back. With every movement of the furious god, the arrows rattled on his shoulders, and his descent was like nightfall. He settled down some way from the ships and shot an arrow, with a terrifying twang from his silver bow. He attacked the mules first and the swift dogs; then he aimed his sharp arrows at the men, and struck again and again. Day and night, packed funeral pyres burned.

For nine days the god's arrows rained down on the camp. On the tenth, Achilles had the men summoned to assembly, an idea the goddess white-armed Hera gave him in her concern for the Greeks whose destruction she was witnessing. When everyone had arrived and the gathering was complete, swift-footed Achilles rose and spoke to them:

'Agamemnon son of Atreus, what with the ravages of the fighting and the plague, any of us that are not dead by then will soon, I think, have to sail for home. Come, let us consult some prophet or priest or some interpreter of dreams (dreams, as you know, are sent by Zeus) and find out from him why Phoebus Apollo is so angry with us. He may be offended at some broken vow

5

or failure in our rites. If so, he may be willing to accept an offering of unblemished sheep and goats and save us from the plague.'

With these words Achilles sat down, and Calchas son of Thestor rose to his feet. As a prophet, Calchas had no rival in the camp. Past, present and future held no secrets from him; and it was his second sight – a gift he owed to Apollo – that had guided the Greek ships to Ilium. He had their interests at heart as he rose and addressed them:

'Achilles dear to Zeus, you have instructed me to account for the anger of lord Apollo the Archer-god; and I will do so. But listen to me first and swear an oath to use all your eloquence and strength to look after me and protect me. I ask this of you, being well aware that I am about to infuriate a man whose authority is great among us and whose word is law to all the Greeks. An ordinary mortal is no match for anyone in authority he angers. Even if his superior swallows his anger for the moment, he will still nurse his grievance till the day when he can settle the account. Consider, then, whether you can guarantee my safety.'

Swift-footed Achilles replied and said:

'Put your mind at rest and tell us everything you have learnt from the god. For by Apollo son of Zeus, the very god to whom you pray, Calchas, when you reveal your prophecies – I swear that as long as I am alive and look on the earth, not one of all the Greeks here by the hollow ships will raise a fist against you, not even if the man you mean is Agamemnon, who now claims to be far the best of all.'

Then the matchless prophet took heart and said:

'Apollo has found no fault with any broken vows or failures in our rites. Agamemnon insulted his priest, did not free his daughter and refused the ransom – that is why Apollo made us suffer and will continue to do so. He will not release us from this loathsome plague till we give the dark-eyed girl back to her father, without recompense or ransom, and send a sacred offering to the priest's town of Chryse. Appease him like that, and we might persuade him to relent.'

With these words Calchas sat down, and the warrior son of Atreus, wide-ruling Agamemnon, leapt up, enraged. His heart seethed with fury, and his eyes were like flames of fire. With a menacing look he spoke first to Calchas:

'Prophet of evil, never yet have you said a word to my advantage. It's always trouble you revel in predicting. Not once have you delivered a positive prophecy – not once! And now you hold forth as the army's prophet, telling the Greeks that the Archer-god Apollo is perse-cuting them because I refused the splendid ransom for the girl Chryseis. And why? Because I wanted to have her at home myself. Indeed, I like her better than my wife Clytaemnestra. Chryseis is quite as beautiful and no less clever or skilful with her hands.

'Still, I am willing to give her up, if that appears the better course. I want my army alive and well, not dead or dying. But give me another prize at once or I will be the only one of us without one. That cannot be right. You can all see for yourselves that the prize I was given is on its way elsewhere.'

7

Swift-footed godlike Achilles replied:

'Most glorious Agamemnon, unequalled in your greed, where will the great-hearted Greeks find you a fresh prize? I have yet to hear of any store of common property we have laid by. The plunder we took from captured towns has been distributed. It cannot be right to ask the men to reassemble that. No: give the girl back now, as the god demands, and we will compensate you three, four times over, if Zeus ever allows us to sack this Trojan town with its fine walls.'

Lord Agamemnon replied and said:

'You are a great warrior, godlike Achilles, but don't imagine you can trick me into that. I am not going to be outmanoeuvred or persuaded by you. "Give up the girl", you say, in order to keep your own prize safe. Do you expect me to sit tamely by, while I am robbed? No: if the army is prepared to give me a fresh prize, they must choose one to my taste to make up for my loss. If not, I shall come and help myself to your prize, or Ajax's, or maybe I shall walk off with Odysseus'. And what an angry man I shall leave behind me!

'However, we can deal with all that later. For the moment, let us run a black ship down into the bright sea, carefully select her crew, load the animals for sacrifice and put the girl herself, fair-cheeked Chryseis, on board. And let some adviser be in charge, Ajax, Idomeneus, godlike Odysseus, or you yourself, Achilles, most impetuous of all Greeks, to offer the sacrifice and win us back Apollo's favour.'

Swift-footed Achilles gave him a black look and replied:

'You shameless, self-centred . . . ! How can you expect any of the men to comply with you willingly when you send them on a raid or into battle? It was no quarrel with Trojan warriors that brought *me* here to fight. They have never done *me* any harm. They have never lifted oxen or horses of mine, nor ravaged my crops back home in fertile Phthia, nurse of warriors. The roaring seas and many a dark range of mountains lie between us.

'We joined your expedition, you shameless swine, to please you, to get satisfaction from the Trojans for Menelaus and yourself, dog-face – a fact you utterly ignore. And now comes this threat from you, of all people, to rob me of my prize, in person, my hard-earned prize which was a tribute from the army. It's not as though I am ever given a prize equal to yours when the Greeks sack some prosperous Trojan town. The heat and burden of the fighting fall on me, but when it comes to dealing out the spoils, it is you that takes the lion's share, leaving me to return to my ships, exhausted from battle, with some pathetic portion to call my own.

'So, I shall now go back home to Phthia. That is the best thing I can do – to sail home with my beaked ships. I can see no point in staying here to be insulted, while I pile up wealth and luxuries for you.'

Agamemnon lord of men replied:

'Run for it, then, by all means, if that's the way you feel. I am not going down on bended knees to entreat you to stay here on my account. There are others with me who will treat me with respect, and Zeus wise in counsel is first among them. Of all the Olympian-bred lords here, you are the most hateful to me. Rivalry, war, fighting – these are the breath of life to you. If you *are* a great warrior, it is because the god made you so. Go home now with your ships and your men-at-arms and rule your Myrmidons. I have no interest in you whatsoever. Your resentment leaves me cold.

'But here is a threat: in the same way as Phoebus Apollo is robbing me of Chryseis, whom I propose to send off in my ship with my crew, I will come in person to your hut and take away fair-cheeked Briseis, your prize, Achilles, to let you know how far I am your superior and to teach others to shrink from claiming parity with me and playing the equal to my face.'

So he spoke, and his words infuriated Achilles. In his manly chest, his heart was torn whether to draw the sharp sword from his side, thrust his way through the crowd and disembowel Agamemnon, or control himself and check his angry impulse. These thoughts were racing through his mind, and he was just drawing his great sword from his sheath when Athene came down from the skies. The goddess white-armed Hera had sent her because she felt equally close to both men and was concerned for them.

Athene stood behind Achilles and seized him by his auburn hair. No one but Achilles was aware of her; the rest saw nothing. Achilles was amazed. He swung round, recognized Pallas Athene at once – so wonderful was the light from her eyes – and spoke winged words:

'Why have you come here this time, daughter of Zeus who drives the storm-cloud? Is it to witness Agamemnon's humiliating affront? I tell you bluntly and, believe me, I mean it: he stands to pay for this insolence with his life.'

The goddess grey-eyed Athene replied:

'I came from the skies to cool your fury, if you will listen to me. The goddess white-armed Hera sent me because she feels equally close to both of you and is concerned for you. Come now, give up this quarrel and take your hand from your sword. Insult him with words instead and tell him what you mean to do. I tell you bluntly and I *do* mean it: the day shall come when splendid gifts three times as valuable as what you have now lost will be laid at your feet because of that humiliating affront. Hold your hand, then, and do as we tell you.'

Swift-footed Achilles replied and said:

'Goddess, a man must respect what you and Hera say, however angry he may be. Better for him if he does. The gods listen to the man who goes along with them.'

He spoke, placed his heavy hand on the silver hilt, drove the long sword back into its scabbard and complied with Athene, who then set out for Olympus and the palace of Zeus who drives the storm-cloud, where she rejoined the other gods.

Not that Achilles curbed his anger. He rounded bitterly on Agamemnon and said:

'You drunkard, you, with your eyes of a dog and heart of a doe! You never have the courage to arm yourself and go into battle with the men, let alone join the pick of the Greeks in an ambush – you'd sooner die. It suits you better to remain in camp, walking off with the prizes of anyone who contradicts you – a leader who grows fat on his own people! But then, you rule over nobodies: otherwise, son of Atreus, this outrage would prove your last.

'But I tell you bluntly, and I am going to take a solemn oath on this staff in my hands. Once cut from its stem in the hills, it can never put out leaves or twigs again. The bronze axe stripped it of its bark and foliage: it will sprout no more. The men who in the name of Zeus safeguard our traditions now hold it when they give judgement. By this I solemnly swear that the day is coming when the Greeks one and all will miss Achilles badly, and you in your despair will be powerless to help them as they fall in their multitudes to man-slaying Hector. Then you will tear your heart out in remorse for giving no respect to the best of the Greeks.'

So spoke the son of Peleus, flung down the staff with its golden studs and resumed his seat, leaving Agamemnon thundering at him from the other side. But Nestor now leapt up, eloquent Nestor, the clear-voiced orator from Pylos whose speech flowed sweeter than honey off his tongue. He had already seen two generations of men born, grow up and die in sacred Pylos, and now he ruled the third. He had their interests at heart as he rose and addressed them:

'What can I say? This is indeed enough to make Greece weep! How happy Priam and his sons would be, how all the Trojans would rejoice, if they could hear you at each other's throats, you, the two best Greeks when it comes to giving advice and fighting!

'Now listen to me. You are both my juniors. What's more, I have mixed in the past with even better men than you and never failed to carry conviction with them, the finest men I have ever seen or shall see, men like Peirithous and Dryas shepherd of the people, Caeneus, Exadius, godlike Polyphemus and Aegeus' son Theseus, a man like the gods. These Lapiths were the strongest men that earth has bred, the strongest men who pitted themselves against the strongest enemies – the mountain-dwelling Centaurs, whom they violently destroyed. These were the men I left my home in Pylos to join. I travelled far to meet them – they invited me, personally – and I fought my own campaign. Not a soul on earth today could live with those men in battle – and they listened to what I said and followed my advice. You two do the same. It's for your own good to go along with what I tell you.

'You, Agamemnon, though you have the authority, do not rob him of his girl. The Greek army gave her to him first. Let him keep his prize. And you, Achilles, give up your desire to cross swords with your leader. Through the authority he derives from Zeus, a leader who holds the sceptre of power has more claim to our respect than anyone else. Even if you, with a goddess for mother, are the better fighter, yet Agamemnon is your superior since he rules more people. Agamemnon, cool your fury; I, Nestor, entreat you to put aside your anger against Achilles who is a mighty tower of strength for every Greek in the hell of battle.'

Lord Agamemnon replied and said:

'Venerable sir, all that is very true. But this man here wants no superiors: he wants to dominate everyone, to

13

lord it over everyone and to give us each our orders, though I know one person who is not going to stand for that. What if the everlasting gods did make a spearman of him? Does that entitle him to hurl insults – ?'

Abruptly, godlike Achilles replied:

'A pathetic little nonentity I shall be called, for sure, if I give in to you at every point, no matter what you say. Issue your commands to the rest. Don't tell me what to do. I have done with taking your orders. And I'll tell you something else, and you bear it in mind. I am not going to fight you, or anyone else, with my bare hands for this girl's sake. You Greeks gave her to me, and now you take her back. But there's much else by my swift black ship that is mine, and you will take none of that against my will. Come on, just try, so that everyone here can see what happens. Your black blood will soon be flowing down my spear.'

The war of words was over. The two stood up and dismissed the assembly by the Greek ships. Achilles, with Menoetius' son Patroclus and his Myrmidon troops, made off to his hut and ships; while Agamemnon launched a swift ship into the water, chose twenty rowers, loaded the offering of cattle for sacrifice to the god and seated fair-cheeked Chryseis on board. Quick-thinking Odysseus went as their leader and, when everyone was aboard, they set off along the highways of the sea.

Meanwhile Agamemnon ordered the army to purify itself by bathing. When they had done this and thrown the dirty water into the waves, they offered perfect sacrifices of bulls and goats to Apollo on the shore of the murmuring sea. The smell of sacrifice, mixed with the curling smoke, went up into the sky.

While the army was engaged on these duties in the camp, Agamemnon did not forget his quarrel with Achilles and the threat he had made at the assembly. He spoke to Talthybius and Eurybates, his heralds and busy attendants:

'Go to Achilles' hut, take fair-cheeked Briseis by the hand and bring her here. If he refuses to let her go, I shall come in force to fetch her myself, which will be all the worse for him.'

So he spoke, and bluntly dismissed them. The two made their unwilling way along the shore of the murmuring sea till they reached the Myrmidons' huts and ships, where they found Achilles himself sitting by his own black ship. It gave him no pleasure to see them. They came to a halt, too terrified and embarrassed before their lord to address him or ask anything. But he realized what was going on and spoke out:

'Heralds, ambassadors of Zeus and men, welcome. Come in. My quarrel is not with you but with Agamemnon, who sent you here to fetch the girl Briseis. Come, Olympian-born Patroclus, bring the girl out and hand her over to these men. I shall count on them to be my witnesses before the blessed gods, before men and before the obstinate Agamemnon as well, if the Greeks ever need me again to save them from some terrible disaster. That man is raving mad, incapable of understanding the past or the future, let alone how the army is going to survive when it's fighting for its life by the ships.'

So he spoke, and Patroclus did as his dear companion had told him, brought out fair-cheeked Briseis from their hut and gave her up to the two men, who made their way back along the line of the ships: the girl went unwillingly with them.

Withdrawing from his men, Achilles broke into tears. He sat down by himself on the shore of the grey sea and looked out across the boundless ocean. Then, stretching out his arms, he poured out prayers to his mother:

'Mother, since you, a goddess, bore me to live the briefest of lives, surely high-thundering Olympian Zeus owes me some measure of respect. But he pays me none – not even a little. Look how wide-ruling Agamemnon son of Atreus has dishonoured me. He took my prize, made off with her in person and now he has her for himself.'

So he spoke in tears, and his lady mother heard him where she sat in the depths of the sea with her old father. She rose swiftly from the grey water like a mist, came and sat by her weeping son, stroked him with her hand and said:

'My child, why these tears? Why this sorrow? Tell me, don't keep it to yourself. We must share it.'

Swift-footed Achilles sighed heavily and said:

'You know and, since you know, why should I tell you the whole story? We went to Thebe, Eëtion's sacred town, sacked it and brought back all the plunder. The sons of the Greeks shared it out among themselves in the proper way and chose fair-cheeked Chryseis for Agamemnon. Then Chryses, priest of the Archer-god Apollo, came to the ships of the bronze-armoured Greeks to recover his captured daughter. He brought with him an immense ransom and carried the emblems of the Archer-god Apollo on a golden staff in his hands. He spoke in supplication to the whole Greek army, and most of all its two commanders, Agamemnon and Menelaus, the sons of Atreus. Then all the other Greeks shouted in agreement. They wanted to see the priest respected and the splendid ransom taken. But this was not at all to Agamemnon's liking. He cruelly and bluntly dismissed the priest.

'So, the old man went back in anger; but Apollo listened to his prayers – the priest was very dear to him – and launched his deadly arrows at the Greek army. The men fell thick and fast, since the god's arrows rained down on every part of the broad Greek camp. At last a prophet who understood the god's will explained the matter to us. I was the first to rise and advise them to appease the god. This made Agamemnon furious. He leapt to his feet and threatened me. And now he has carried out his threats. The dark-eyed Greeks are taking Chryseis to Chryse in a swift ship with offerings for the god, while Agamemnon's heralds have just gone from my hut with the girl Briseis, whom the army gave to me.

'So now, if you have any power, protect your son. Go to Olympus and, if anything you have ever said or done has warmed the heart of Zeus, remind him of it as you supplicate him. For instance, in my father's house I often heard you proudly telling us how you alone among the gods once saved Zeus who darkens the clouds from a terrible disaster when some of the other Olympians – Hera, Poseidon and Pallas Athene – had plotted to throw him in chains. You, goddess, went and had him released. You immediately summoned to high Olympus that monster with a hundred arms – the gods call him Briareus, but mankind Aegaeon – a giant more powerful even than his father. He took up his position beside Zeus son of Cronus, exulting in his glory, and the blessed gods slunk off in terror, leaving Zeus free.

'Sit by him now, take him by the knees and remind him of that. Persuade him, if you can, to help the Trojans and to fling the Greeks back on their ships, pen them hard against the sea and massacre them. That would teach them the true measure of their leader. Make wide-ruling Agamemnon son of Atreus realize the delusion he is under in giving no respect to the best of all the Greeks.'

Thetis replied in tears:

'My son, my son! Cursed in my child-bearing, was it for this I nursed you? If only you could have been left to pass your days without tears or trouble beside the ships, since destiny has given you so short a life, no time at all. As it is, you are not only doomed to an early death but also to a most miserable life. It was indeed to an evil destiny that I brought you into the world.

'Nevertheless, I will go to snow-capped Olympus to tell all this myself to Zeus who delights in thunder, and I will see whether I can move him. Meanwhile, stay by your swift ships, keep up your anger against the Greeks and take no part in the fighting. Yesterday, I must tell you, Zeus left for Ocean to join the matchless Ethiopians at a feast, and all the gods went with him. But in twelve days' time he will be back on Olympus, and then I shall go to his bronze-floored palace where I will fall on my knees at his feet. I am convinced he will do what I ask.'

With these words she departed and left Achilles there, anger mounting in his heart at the treatment of his well-girdled woman Briseis, whom they had taken from him against his will.

Meanwhile Odysseus and his crew reached Chryse with the sacred offerings. When they had brought their ship into the waters of the deep-bayed port, they gathered up the sails and stowed them in the black ship's hold, quickly slackened the forestays, dropped the mast into its crutch, rowed the ship into her moorings, threw out anchor-stones from the prow into the sea, tied up the stern hawsers on land and disembarked on to the beach. The cattle for the Archer-god Apollo were landed, and Chryseis stepped ashore from the seafaring vessel. Quick-thinking Odysseus then led the girl to the altar, gave her back into her father's arms and said:

'Chryses, Agamemnon lord of men has ordered me to bring you your daughter and to make a sacred offering of oxen to Apollo on the Greeks' behalf, in the hope of pacifying the god who has been inflicting sorrow and mourning on our men.'

With these words he handed the girl over into the arms of her father, who joyfully welcomed his beloved child.

The sacred offering of oxen to do honour to the god was quickly set in place round the well-built altar. The men rinsed their hands and took up the sacrificial grains. Then Chryses lifted up his hands and prayed aloud:

'Hear me, Apollo, lord of the silver bow, protector

of Chryse and holy Cilla, mighty ruler over Tenedos! You heard me when I prayed to you before; you showed your respect for me and struck a great blow at the Greek army. Now grant me a second wish and lift the loathsome plague from the Greeks.'

So he spoke in prayer, and Phoebus Apollo heard him. When they had made their prayers and thrown the grain over the victims, they first drew back the animals' heads, slit their throats and skinned them. Then, for the god's portion, they cut out the thigh bones, wrapped them in folds of fat and laid raw meat from the rest of the animal above them. These pieces the old priest burnt on wooden spits while he poured libations of red wine over them and the young men gathered round him with five-pronged forks in their hands. When the god's portion had been consumed by fire, they ate the offal and then carved the rest of the victims into small pieces, pierced them with skewers, roasted them carefully and drew them all off.

When their work was done and the meal prepared, they feasted, and no one went without a fair share. Their hunger and thirst satisfied, the young men filled the mixing-bowls to the brim with wine and went round the whole company, pouring some into each cup for a libation to the god. And for the rest of the day the young Greek warriors sang and danced to appease the god with a beautiful hymn celebrating the Archer Apollo, to which he listened with delight.

When the sun set and darkness fell, they lay down to sleep by the hawsers of their ship. But when early-born, rosy-fingered Dawn appeared, they set sail for the broad

Greek camp, taking advantage of a favourable breeze the Archer-god had sent them. They put up their mast and spread the white sail. The wind filled its belly, and a dark wave hissed loudly round her keel as the vessel gathered way and sped through the swell, forging ahead on her course. So they returned to the broad Greek camp, where they dragged the black ship high up on the sandy shore and kept it upright with wooden props. That done, they dispersed to their several huts and ships.

But Olympian-born son of Peleus swift-footed Achilles was sitting by his ships, nursing his anger. He had not only kept away from the fighting but had attended no meetings of the assembly where men win glory. He stayed where he was, eating his heart out and longing for the sound and fury of battle.

Eleven days went by, and at dawn on the twelfth the everlasting gods returned in full strength to Olympus, with Zeus at their head. Thetis, remembering her son's instructions, emerged in the morning from the waves of the sea, rose into the broad sky and reached Olympus. She found far-thundering Zeus sitting away from the rest of the gods on the highest of Olympus' many peaks. She sank down in front of him, put her left arm round his knees, took his chin in her right hand and in supplication spoke to lord Zeus son of Cronus:

'Father Zeus, if ever I have served you well among the gods by word or deed, grant me this wish: give honour to my son. He is already singled out for an early death, and now Agamemnon lord of men has dishonoured him. He took his prize, removed her in person and now he has her for himself. But you at least do him honour, Olympian Zeus wise in counsel, and let the Trojans have the upper hand till the Greeks pay back my son and increase the honour in which he is held.'

So she spoke, and Zeus who marshals the clouds made no reply. He sat in silence for a long time, with Thetis clinging to his knees as she had done throughout. Then she asked once more:

'Promise me faithfully and bow your head in agreement, or else, since you have nothing to fear by doing so, refuse; then I shall know for sure that no other god is less respected than I am.'

Much perturbed, Zeus who marshals the clouds replied:

'This is going to mean trouble! You will make me fall foul of my wife Hera when she heaps me with abuse for this, as she will. Even as things are, she slanders me constantly before the other gods and accuses me of helping the Trojans in this war.

'However, leave me now, or Hera may notice us; and I will see the matter through. But first, to reassure you, I will bow my head in agreement – and the immortals recognize no surer guarantee from me than that. When I seal a promise with a nod, there can be no failure to fulfil it, no going back, no deception.'

The son of Cronus spoke and nodded his sable brows. The divine locks rolled forward from the lord god's immortal head, and great Olympus shook.

The agreement was made, and the two now parted. Thetis plunged down from glittering Olympus into the salt-sea depths, while Zeus departed for his own palace. There the whole company of gods rose from their seats in their Father's presence. There was no one that dared to keep his seat as he approached; they all stood up as he came in.

So Zeus sat down on his throne; and Hera had seen, and knew that he and silver-footed Thetis, daughter of the Old Man of the Sea, had hatched a plot between them. At once she spoke to Zeus with cutting words:

'Which god has been hatching plots with you this time, you arch-deceiver? How like you it is to wait till my back is turned and then cook up some secret schemes, on your own. You have never been willing to confide in me.'

The Father of men and gods replied to her:

'Hera, don't expect to learn all my decisions. You would find the knowledge hard to bear, although you are my wife. What it is right for you to hear, no man or god shall know before you. But when I choose to take a step without referring to the gods, don't cross-examine me about it.'

Ox-eyed lady Hera replied:

'Dread son of Cronus, what are you suggesting now? Surely it was never my way to pester you with questions; you are at liberty to make whatever decisions you like. But now I have a terrible fear you have been talked round by silver-footed Thetis, daughter of the Old Man of the Sea. She sat with you this morning and took you by the knees. This makes me suppose you have given your word to her to honour Achilles and let the Greeks be slaughtered in their multitudes by their ships.'

Zeus who marshals the clouds replied and said:

'Remarkable! You can never stop "supposing". I can keep no secrets from you. But there is nothing you can *do* – except to turn me even more against you, which will be all the worse for yourself. If things are as you say, you may take it that my will is being done. Sit there in silence and obey me, or all the gods on Olympus will be of no help in keeping me off when I lay my unconquerable hands on you.'

So he spoke, and ox-eyed lady Hera was afraid and, restraining her feelings, sat down in silence. The Sky-gods in Zeus' palace were filled with consternation, till at last the great craftsman Hephaestus, who sided with his mother white-armed Hera, began to address them:

'This is going to mean trouble, and we are not going to put up with it, with you two squabbling over mere mortals and setting the gods at loggerheads. It will be impossible to enjoy a good feast with so much trouble in the air. I do advise my mother, who knows well enough what is best, to make her peace with my dear Father Zeus, or she may draw another rebuke from him and the feast be entirely spoilt. If he wanted to, the Olympian lord of the lightning flash, our superior by far, could blast us all from our seats. No, Mother, deal with him tactfully, and the Olympian will be gracious to us again.'

So he spoke, hurried forward with a two-handled cup, put it in his mother's hands and said:

'Mother, be patient and swallow your resentment, or, much as I love you, I may see you thrashed here in front of me. A distressing sight for me, but I will be unable to do anything to help you. The Olympian is a hard god to resist. Why, once before, when I was trying to save you, he seized me by the foot and hurled me from the threshold of Olympus. I flew all day and, as the sun sank, I fell, all the life knocked out of me, on Lemnos, where I was picked up and looked after by the Sintians.'

So he spoke, and the goddess white-armed Hera smiled and took the cup from her son, still smiling. Then Hephaestus went on to serve the rest in turn, beginning from the left, with sweet nectar which he drew from the mixing bowl; and a fit of helpless laughter seized the blessed gods as they watched him bustling up and down the hall.

So the feast went on, all day till sundown. No one went short of the pleasures of food or music: Apollo played his magnificent lyre and the Muses sang, voice answering glorious voice. But when the bright lamp of the sun had set, they all went home to bed in the separate houses that the famous lame god Hephaestus with his supreme skill had built for them. Olympian Zeus, lord of the lightning flash, retired to the bed where he usually rested when sweet sleep overcame him. There he went up and slept, with Hera of the golden throne beside him.

The Embassy to Achilles (Book 9)

The Trojans, led by their champion Hector, are threatening the Greek camp. Many Greek heroes have been wounded in the fighting.

While the Trojans kept their watch, the Greek army was haunted by panic and chilling thoughts of flight. All their leaders were overwhelmed with inconsolable grief at their losses. As the north and west winds suddenly descend from Thrace to whip up the teeming sea; white horses cap the darkening rollers, and seaweed piles up all along the beach – so Greek morale was shattered.

Agamemnon, wandering about in complete despair, told his clear-voiced heralds to summon every man by name to an assembly, but not to call out loud and alert the Trojans. He himself played a leading part in this task. The men sat down to the assembly in some desperation. Agamemnon rose, weeping tears like a dark spring trickling black streaks of water down a steep rock-face. Sighing heavily, he addressed the Greeks:

'Friends, rulers and leaders of the Greeks, Zeus son of Cronus has seriously deluded me, a crushing blow. That perverse god once solemnly assured me that we would sack Ilium with its fine walls and return home; but now his advice turns out to be an evil deception, and he is telling me to return home to Argos in disgrace, with half my army lost. It appears that this is what almighty Zeus, who has brought down the high towers of many a town and will destroy others yet, has decided, such is his absolute power. So I suggest we all do what I now propose – board ship and home to the land of our fathers! The Trojans' town with its broad streets will never fall to us.'

So he spoke and was received in complete silence by them all. For a long time everyone sat there, speechless and dejected. Eventually Diomedes, master of the battle-cry, spoke out:

'Agamemnon son of Atreus, I will begin by taking issue with you over your stupid proposal – here in open assembly, commander, as is normal practice – and you must not be offended.

'You took it on yourself the other day to call my courage in question in front of the troops. You said I was a weakling and a coward. Well, every Greek, young and old, knows how far *that* is the case. Then again, Zeus, son of sickle-wielding Cronus, has granted you some things, but not others. He gave you the sceptre of power and the honour it brings with it, but he did not give you courage – and courage is the secret of authority. You amaze me – do you really believe the Greeks are the cowards and weaklings you say they are? If you, for one, have set your heart on getting away, then go. The way is clear, and all your ships are drawn up by the sea, the whole great fleet of them that brought you from Mycenae. But the rest of the long-haired Greeks are going to stay till we conquer Troy. Or let them scramble back home in their ships as well. We two, I and my charioteer Sthenelus, will fight on till we reach our goal in Ilium. We are here because the god wants us to be.'

So he spoke, and all the Greeks shouted their approval, delighted at the words of horse-taming Diomedes. Now the charioteer Nestor rose to speak: 'Diomedes, you are a formidable warrior in a fight, and in debate you have no rival of your age; no one here will object to your speech or contradict a word of it. But it was beside the point. You certainly talked sensibly to the Greek leaders in terms appropriate to your age, but you are a young man – there's no denying it – and in fact you could be my youngest son. But I am much older than you are, and it is now time for me to speak out and take the whole situation into consideration. And no one will look down on what I have to say, not even lord Agamemnon; for that man is indeed an outlaw from clan, law and home who is in love with the bitter taste of internal discord.

'For the moment, we must take the night into account and eat. Sentries must be posted at intervals along the ditch outside the wall. That is a duty I leave to the younger men. After that, Agamemnon, since you rank the highest here, you must take the initiative. Invite your senior advisers to a feast. It is the right way to proceed and can do you no harm. Day by day Greek ships bring wine to you over the broad seas from Thrace. Your huts are full of it; and as ruler over many people, it is for you to offer hospitality. When you have gathered us all together, you must listen to the man who gives you the best advice. We Greeks certainly all need the best and most reliable we can get, with all those Trojan camp-fires so close to our ships. Who finds *them* a pleasant sight? This one night will sink or save the whole expedition.'

So he spoke, and they heard and agreed. Armed sentries went out at the double under the command of Nestor's son Thrasymedes shepherd of the people; Ascalaphus and Ialmenus, children of the War-god; Meriones, Aphareus, and Deipyrus; and godlike Lycomedes, Creon's son. There were seven captains of the guard, and a hundred young men marched behind each, armed with long spears. They took their posts midway between the ditch and the wall, where each contingent lit a fire and laid out food.

Meanwhile Agamemnon led the whole party of senior advisers to his huts and had a heartening meal served up. They helped themselves to the good things spread before them and, when their hunger and thirst were satisfied, the old man Nestor, whose wisdom had won the day before, expounded his plan. He had their interests at heart as he rose and addressed them:

'Most glorious Agamemnon son of Atreus, lord of men, with you my speech begins and it will end with you. You are ruler over many people, for whose guidance Zeus granted you the sceptre and the authority to take decisions. So you, above all, must both give and listen to advice and carry out the suggestions that others may feel bound to put forward in the common interest. You will get the credit, whatever the proposal.

'Now I will tell you how things seem to me – because no one will come up with a better analysis than mine. I formed it at the time and have not altered it, since the moment, Olympian-born Agamemnon, you infuriated

29

Achilles by going to take the young girl Briseis from his hut. We were all against it; and I for one did my best to dissuade you. But your arrogant temper got the better of you, and you dishonoured a man of the highest distinction, whom the gods themselves respected, by taking and keeping his prize. Even at this late hour, then, we should consider how to talk him round and appease him with soothing gifts and winning words.'

Agamemnon lord of men replied:

'Venerable sir, your account of my blind folly is the truth. Deluded I was – I for one cannot deny it. The man Zeus takes to his heart and honours – as he now does that man to the point of crushing the Greeks – is worth a whole army. But since I gave in to a lamentable impulse and committed this act of blind folly, I am willing to make amends and give him limitless compensation.

'Before you all, I list the prestigious gifts I have in mind: seven tripods untarnished by the flames; ten talents of gold; twenty cauldrons of gleaming copper; and twelve powerful racehorses whose speed has made winners of them. Why, with nothing more than the prizes they have won for me, a man would not be badly off or short of precious gold.

'I will give him seven women skilled in arts and crafts, women of exceptional beauty that I chose out of the spoils when he captured thriving Lesbos. I will give him these and, with them, the woman I took from him, the daughter of Briseus. Moreover, I shall give him my solemn oath that I have never been in her bed and slept with her, as men and women do. All these gifts shall be put in his hands at once.

'Later, if the gods permit us to sack Priam's great town, let him come in with us when we are sharing out the spoils, load his ship with gold and bronze to his heart's content, and pick out twenty Trojan women for himself, the loveliest he can find after Greek Helen.

'And if in due course we get back to Argos, the most fertile of all lands, he can become my son-in-law, and I will honour him as I do Orestes, my beloved son, who is being brought up there in the lap of luxury. I have three daughters in my strong palace, Chrysothemis, Laodice and Iphianassa. Of these he shall choose for his own whichever he likes best and take her back to Peleus' house, without the usual bride-gifts. Indeed, I will give *him* gifts, generous ones, more than anyone has ever given with his daughter.

'Not only that, but I will give him seven prosperous towns: Cardamyle, Enope and grassy Hire; holy Pherae and Antheia with its deep meadows; beautiful Aepeia and Pedasus rich in vines. They are all near the sea, in the farthest part of sandy Pylos. Their people are rich in flocks and cattle. They will honour him with their gifts as though he were a god and, being under his authority, give him rich dues.

'All this I will do for him the moment he abandons his anger. Let him surrender. We all know it is because Hades is so implacable and unyielding that he is more hated by mortals than any other god. Yes, let him submit to me, since I rank higher than he does and am older as well.'

Nestor the Gerenian charioteer replied:

'Most glorious Agamemnon son of Atreus, lord of

31

men, nobody could say your offer to lord Achilles was not generous. Very well then, we must now send an urgent deputation to Achilles' hut. I will nominate the men myself, and they must not refuse the duty. First of all Phoenix, dear to the gods, must lead the way, then great Ajax and godlike Odysseus. Of the heralds, Odius and Eurybates are the men to go with them. Now fetch water for our hands and call for silence, so that we can pray to Zeus son of Cronus and ask him to have pity on us.'

So he spoke, and everything he said met with their approval. Heralds at once poured water over their hands, and the young men filled the mixing-bowls to the brim with wine and went round the whole company, pouring some into each cup for a libation to the god. When they had poured their libations and drunk as much as they wished, the envoys set out from Agamemnon's hut. Glancing from one man to another, but with an especial eye for Odysseus, Nestor gave them full instructions to do their utmost to win over matchless Achilles.

They walked together along the shore of the sounding sea with many a prayer to the earthshaker Poseidon who encircles the world that it might be easy to win over Achilles' proud heart. When they came to the Myrmidons' huts and ships, they found him entertaining himself on a tuneful lyre, a beautifully ornate instrument with a silver crossbar which he had taken from the spoils when he destroyed Eëtion's town. With this he was entertaining himself, singing of the famous deeds of heroes. He was alone but for Patroclus, who was sitting opposite him in silence, waiting for him to stop singing.

The envoys drew near, godlike Odysseus leading, and halted in front of him. Achilles was amazed, sprang to his feet still holding his lyre and came forward from the chair where he had been sitting. Patroclus too got up when he saw the men. Extending his hand, swift-footed Achilles said:

'Welcome – to my dear friends! Something urgent must have brought you here, you who are dearest of all the Greeks to me, however angry I am with them.'

With these words godlike Achilles led them into his hut and seated them on chairs with purple coverings. Then he turned quickly to Patroclus, who was standing nearby, and said:

'Bring out a bigger bowl, Patroclus, mix less water with the wine and give every man a cup. Here are my dearest friends under my own roof.'

So he spoke, and Patroclus did as his companion asked. He put down a hefty chopping-block in the firelight, and laid on it the backs of a sheep and a plump goat and the lower back of a great hog, rich in fat. Automedon held these for him while Achilles jointed them and then carved up the joints and spitted the slices. Meanwhile, Patroclus stoked up the fire. When it had burnt down and the flames had died away, he spread out the embers and laid the spits above them, resting them on the supports, after he had sprinkled the meat with salt. When he had roasted it and heaped it up on platters, Patroclus fetched some bread and set it out on the table in handsome baskets; and Achilles divided the meat into portions. This done, Achilles took a chair by the wall opposite godlike Odysseus

and told his companion Patroclus to sacrifice to the gods.
Patroclus threw the ritual pieces on the fire, and they all
helped themselves to the good things spread before them.
Their hunger and thirst satisfied, Ajax nodded to Phoe-
nix. But godlike Odysseus caught the signal and, having
filled his cup with wine, drank to Achilles:

'Your health, Achilles! With all these appetizing dishes
set before us we are certainly not short of our share of
feasts, either in Agamemnon's hut or here again in yours.

'But at the moment the pleasures of the table are far
from our thoughts. We are staring disaster in the face,
Olympian-bred Achilles, and the prospect appals us.
Unless *you* put on a show of force, it is in the balance
whether our ships will be saved or destroyed.

'The proud Trojans and their famous allies have taken
up positions right next to the ships and our defensive
wall. Their camp is bright with fires. They are convinced
there is now nothing left to stop them from falling on the
vessels. Zeus son of Cronus showers them with favour-
able omens, his lightning flashing on the right.

'And Hector is running wild, elated and irresistible.
He puts complete trust in Zeus and respects neither man
nor god in the mad-dog frenzy that possesses him. His
one prayer is for the goddess Dawn to break at once,
when he is promising to hack the peaks from the sterns
of our ships as trophies, see the ships devoured by fire,
smoke us out and slaughter us by the hulls. My big fear
is the gods will let him carry out his threats – that it may
be our destiny to perish here in Troy, far from Greece
where the horses graze.

'Up with you then, if even at this late hour you want to rescue the exhausted troops from the Trojans' fury. You for one will regret it later when disaster has finally struck, since there will be no way of finding a remedy. Give some thought, before that stage is reached, to saving the Greeks from catastrophe.

'My old friend, when your father Peleus sent you from Phthia to join Agamemnon, he gave you this advice: "My son, Athene and Hera, if that is their will, are going to give you the strength. What *you* must do is keep a firm grip on that proud spirit of yours. Fellow feeling is better. Avoid destructive quarrels, and Greeks young and old will look up to you all the more."

'That was the old man's advice – which you have forgotten. But late as it is, yield, now. Give up this heart-rending anger. Agamemnon is ready to make you ample compensation the moment you relent. If you will listen, I will enumerate the gifts he promised in his hut:

'Seven tripods untarnished by the flames; ten talents of gold; twenty cauldrons of gleaming copper; and twelve powerful racehorses whose speed has made winners of them. With nothing more than the prizes they have won, a man would not be badly off or short of precious gold.

'He will give you seven women skilled in arts and crafts, women of exceptional beauty that he chose out of the spoils when you captured thriving Lesbos. He will give you these and, with them, the woman he took from you, the daughter of Briseus. Moreover, he will give you a solemn oath that he has never been in her bed and slept

35

with her, my lord, as men and women do. All these gifts shall be put in your hands at once.

'Later, if the gods permit us to sack Priam's great town, you can go in with them when they are sharing out the spoils, load your ship with gold and bronze to your heart's content and pick out twenty Trojan women for yourself, the loveliest you can find after Greek Helen.

'And if in due course we get back to Argos, the most fertile of all lands, you can become his son-in-law, and he will honour you as he does Orestes, his beloved son, who is being brought up there in the lap of luxury. He has three daughters in his strong palace, Chrysothemis, Laodice and Iphianassa. Of these you can choose for your own whichever you like best and take her back to Peleus' house, without the usual bride-gifts. Indeed, he will give *you* gifts, generous ones, more than anyone has ever given with his daughter.

'Not only that, but he will give you seven prosperous towns: Cardamyle, Enope and grassy Hire; holy Pherae and Antheia with its deep meadows; beautiful Aepeia and Pedasus rich in vines. They are all near the sea, in the farthest part of sandy Pylos. Their people are rich in flocks and cattle. They will honour you with their gifts as though you were a god and, being under your authority, give you rich dues.

'All this he will do for you, the moment you abandon your anger. But if your loathing of Agamemnon, gifts and all, outweighs every other consideration, at least take pity on the Greeks in their camp. They are ready to drop and will honour you like a god. Indeed, you would cover yourself with glory in their eyes, since now you could even kill Hector himself. He reckons he has no equal among all the Greeks whom the ships brought here and he may even come within range of you, in the grip of his destructive madness.'

Swift-footed Achilles replied and said:

'Olympian-born son of Laertes, resourceful Odysseus, I had better tell you point-blank how I feel and what I am going to do, because I don't want relays of you coming here, sitting down and whining and whimpering on at me. I loathe like Hades' gates the man who thinks one thing and says another. So now I will tell you how I see matters.

'I don't think Agamemnon son of Atreus or the rest of the Greeks will win me over, since all along men have been given no reward for battling relentlessly with the enemy day in, day out.

'The man who stays put gets the same share as the man who fights his best. Cowards and brave men are given equal respect. The same death awaits the man who does much, and the man who does nothing.

'All I have suffered by constantly risking my life in battle has left me no better off than anyone else. As a bird brings every morsel she finds to her unfledged chicks, however hard it goes with *her*, so I have spent many a sleepless night and fought through many a bloody day, battling with men for the sake of women.

'Look: I have captured twelve towns by sea and eleven by land across fertile Troy. From each of them I won a magnificent haul of treasure, the whole of which I brought back every time and gave to Agamemnon. To the son of Atreus! Who had stayed put, by the ships. And I'd hand it all over, and he'd take it and dole it out in little bits here and there, and keep the lion's share for himself. Our leading men still have the prizes he gave them, safe and sound in their possession. I am the only one he has robbed, the *only* one. And he has taken the wife I love, too. Well, he can have her – to his heart's content.

'Why do the Greeks have to fight the Trojans? Well, why did the son of Atreus raise an army and bring it here? Was it not for lovely-haired Helen? So are they the only men on earth who love their wives, these sons of Atreus? No, every decent, right-minded man loves and cherishes his own woman, as I loved that girl with all my heart, even though she was a war-captive. But now he has snatched my prize from my arms and cheated me, don't let him try his tricks on me again. I know him too well. He won't win me over.

'No, Odysseus, he'd better work out with you and the rest of the leadership how to save the ships from going up in flames. After all, he has already done *miracles* without me. Look, he's built a wall and dug a ditch along it, a fine broad ditch, complete with stakes! But even so he cannot keep mighty, man-slaying Hector out. Why, in the days when I took the field with the Greeks, nothing would have induced Hector to start a fight any distance at all from the town walls. He'd come no farther than the Scaean gate and the oak-tree – though once he *did* wait for me there on my own and only just escaped with his life.

'But as it is, I now have no desire to fight godlike

Hector. So tomorrow I am going to sacrifice to Zeus and all the other gods, then load and launch my ships. First thing in the morning, if you want to and are interested, you will see my ships crossing the teeming Hellespont and my men straining at the oar. And in three days, given a good crossing by Poseidon, I will be home in fertile Phthia. I have great wealth there which I left behind when, to my cost, I came here; and now I will enrich it further by what I bring back – the gold, the red copper, the well-girdled women and the grey iron that fell to me as my ordinary share of booty, for what it is worth. But *the* prize he gave me, he humiliatingly withdrew – that's what lord Agamemnon did to me, that son of Atreus.

'Tell him all I say and tell him in public. Then the rest of the army can make their feelings clear when he tries to cheat any other Greek. He is utterly shameless, but still the dog cannot even bring himself to look me in the eye. He'll get no advice or action from me. He has cheated me and played me false. He won't take me in again. Once is enough. He can go to hell in his own good time. Zeus wise in counsel has removed his brains.

'I hate his gifts and value *him* at one splinter. Not if he gave me ten or twenty times as much as he possesses or could raise elsewhere, or all the revenues of Orchomenus or Thebes – Egyptian Thebes where the houses are stuffed with treasure, and through every one of a hundred gates two hundred warriors ride out with their chariots and horses – not if he gave me gifts numerous as grains of sand or specks of dust, would Agamemnon ever win me over, until he has paid back the whole heart-rending insult.

'I'm marrying no daughter of Agamemnon son of Atreus. She could be as lovely as golden Aphrodite and as skilful as grey-eyed Athene. I would still not marry her. He can choose some other Greek for her, someone on his own exalted plane, more elevated than me. If the gods allow me to get safely home, my father Peleus will, I am sure, find me a wife. Up and down Hellas and Phthia there are plenty of Greek girls, daughters of nobles who protect their towns. I have only to choose the one I want and make her my own. There were often times at home when my heart's one desire was to make some well-matched girl my lawful wife and enjoy the fortune my old father Peleus had made.

'For nothing, as I now see it, equals the value of life – not the wealth they say prosperous Ilium possessed in earlier days, when there was peace, before the coming of the Greeks, nor all the treasure piled up behind the stone threshold of Phoebus Apollo in rocky Delphi. Cattle and fat sheep can be lifted. Tripods and chestnut horses can be procured. But you cannot lift or procure a man's life, when once the breath has left his lips.

'My divine mother, silver-footed Thetis, says that destiny has left two courses open to me on my journey to the grave. If I stay here and fight it out round Ilium, there is no home-coming for me, but there will be eternal glory instead. If I go back to the land of my fathers, my heroic glory will be forfeit, but my life will be long and I shall be spared an early death.

'And another thing: I would encourage all the rest of you to sail for home too. You are never going to reach your goal in the steep streets of Ilium. Far-thundering Zeus has stretched out a protecting hand over that town, and its people have taken heart.

'So leave me now and report my message to the Greek leaders, freely, as is the privilege of advisers. Then they can think up some better way of saving the ships and all their troops beside them, since this plan, which they thought up as a result of my implacable anger, will not work. But Phoenix can stay here and spend the night with us. Then he can embark for home with me in the morning, if he wants to. There will be no compulsion.'

So he spoke, and was received in complete silence by them all. The bluntness of his words had taken them completely by surprise. Eventually the old charioteer Phoenix spoke up, bursting into tears, so afraid was he for the Greek ships:

'Glorious Achilles, if you really are thinking of sailing home and are so obsessed by your anger that you refuse to save the ships from going up in flames, what is to become of me without you, dear child? How could I possibly stay here, alone? Your father Peleus made me your guardian when he sent you off from Phthia to join Agamemnon. You were a mere boy then with no experience of war, that great leveller, or of debate where men make their mark. It was to teach you all these things, to make a speaker of you and a man of action, that he sent me with you. But I could not bring myself to be separated from you, dear child, not even if the god promised to strip off my years and turn me into the fine young man I was when I first left Hellas with its lovely women.

'I ran away because of a quarrel with my father, Amyntor. His anger with me was down to a lovely-haired woman he intended to bring home. He was passionate about her, which was humiliating for his wife, my mother. So my mother entreated me to sleep with the woman first, and thus make her dislike the old man. I consented and did so. My father guessed at once and with solemn curses called on the hateful Furies to make me childless, so he would never have to lift a son of mine on to his lap; and over time the gods, Zeus of the underworld and august Persephone, fulfilled his curses.

'I then planned to put my father to the sword. But one of the gods restrained me. He made me think of public opinion and of the reproaches I would incur, and how the Greeks must not know me as a father-killer. After that, I could not bring myself to remain any longer in my angry father's house. Naturally, my kinsmen and cousins were all for keeping me there at home and gathered round in entreaty, pleading hard with me. Many fat sheep and shambling cattle with crooked horns were slaughtered; many a fine fat hog was spitted over the flames for singeing; and many a jar of the old man's wine was drunk.

'For nine nights they camped beside me, taking it in turns to go on guard, and keeping two fires burning, one under the colonnade of the walled yard, and the other in the forecourt outside the door of my sleeping-quarters. But on the tenth dark night I broke open the close-fitting doors of my bedroom and escaped. I easily cleared the courtyard wall, and not one of the men or waiting-women on guard saw me. Then I fled far across spacious

Hellas and came as a suppliant to fertile Phthia, mother of flocks, and your father lord Peleus. He welcomed me warmly and loved me as a father loves his son, an only, cherished son, heir to a great estate. He made me a rich man and gave me a populous district to rule, and I settled down on the borders of Phthia as lord of the Dolopes.

'Since then, godlike Achilles, all my loving devotion has gone into making you the great man you are. You would refuse to go out to a feast or touch your food at home unless I was there; I always had to take you on my knees and feed you, cutting up your meat for you and holding the wine to your lips. You would often soak the front of my tunic, dribbling wine all down it – just like a baby! Yes, I went through a great deal for you and worked myself to the bone, aware that the gods were not going to send me a son of my own. So I tried to make *you* my son, godlike Achilles, so that you would save me some day from a miserable end.

'Master your tremendous pride, Achilles. You have no need to be so stubborn. Even the gods themselves, for all their greater majesty, honour and power, are capable of being swayed. When someone has gone too far and done wrong, they supplicate gods with sacrifice and soft prayers, libations and burnt-offerings, to turn them from their anger.

'There are goddesses of supplication, Litae, daughters of almighty Zeus. These Litae are wrinkled creatures, limping, eyes askance, who make it their business to pursue Delusion. But Delusion is strong and sure-footed, because she is quick enough to leave them all behind.

Roaming the world, Delusion brings mankind to grief. But the Litae come after and put the trouble right. The man who respects these daughters of Zeus when they approach him is greatly blessed by them, and they listen to his prayers. But when a man hardens his heart and rebuffs them, they go and supplicate Zeus, asking that Delusion accompany the man so that he comes to grief and pays the price.

'This applies to you, Achilles. You must give the daughters of Zeus that same respect that bends even great men to yield. If Agamemnon had not made you a generous offer with the promise of more to come, but had persisted in his vindictiveness, I would not be asking you to cast your anger to the winds and help the Greeks now, however great their need. But as it is, he is not only offering you a great deal now but guaranteeing much more, as well as choosing the most distinguished men from the whole army to come and supplicate you, men who are your own dearest friends among the Greeks. Don't scorn their message or their mission here – though up till now, no one could have blamed you in the slightest for your anger.

'We all know famous stories of the past when great heroes behaved like this and worked themselves up into a fury of rage, yet proved amenable to gifts and yielded to persuasion. I can remember a case myself from long ago. It's nothing new, but we're all friends here. I'll tell you the story.

'The Curetes were fighting the warlike Aetolians at the town of Calydon, and losses were heavy on both sides. The Aetolians were defending their lovely town of Calydon, and the Curetes doing all they could to sack it. The trouble had been started by the goddess of the golden throne Artemis. She had taken offence when lord Oeneus of Calydon had failed to make her any harvest-offering on the sacred hill in his estate. All the other gods enjoyed rich sacrifices; it was only this daughter of great Zeus to whom he offered nothing. Perhaps he forgot her, perhaps he did not intend to do it – in either case, it was a seriously deluded act.

'In her rage, Artemis who delights in arrows launched at him a foaming wild boar with flashing tusks, which settled down to do much damage, ravaging Oeneus' orchards. It strewed the ground with the tall trees it brought tumbling down, rooting them up, fruit and all. But at last Oeneus' son Meleager killed it. He had to raise huntsmen and hounds from many towns to do this, since the beast was far too powerful to be dealt with by just a few – even so, it still laid many of them on the sad funeral pyre. But then Artemis started the hue and cry of battle over the destination of the carcass: she set the Curetes and Aetolians at each other's throats over who should be awarded the prize of the beast's head and shaggy hide.

'In the war that ensued, as long as Meleager was in the battlefield, things went badly for the Curetes who were unable to hold their ground outside Calydon's walls, for all their numbers. But many a sensible man at times finds his heart swelling with rage, and this is what happened to Meleager now. He got into a fury with his mother Althaea, withdrew from the fighting and stayed at home with his wife, lovely Cleopatra.

'(Cleopatra's mother was slim-ankled Marpessa, and her father was Idas, in his time the strongest man on earth. Phoebus Apollo once snatched Marpessa away, and Idas took on Apollo with his bow to defend his wife's honour. When she had been seized by the Archer-god Apollo, Marpessa mourned as a kingfisher does its mate; and that is why, later, Marpessa and Idas had given Cleopatra the nickname Alcyone, kingfisher, because of her mother.)

'Anyway, Meleager took to his bed with Cleopatra and nursed his heart-rending anger. This anger had been caused by his mother Althaea's curses. Meleager had quarrelled with Althaea's brother, his uncle, over who should get the prize from the boar-hunt and killed him. So his mother in her grief had begged the gods to kill her son Meleager, falling on her knees, deluging her lap with tears and beating the bountiful earth with her fists as she called on Hades and august Persephone. And the Fury that walks in the dark heard her from Hell, and his heart was implacable.

'So before long there arose the noise and commotion of the Curetes at the town gates, battering at the walls. And now the Aetolian elders supplicated Meleager to come out and fight. They sent him a deputation of the leading priests and promised him a great gift. They told him he could choose an estate of fifty acres for his own use, half vineland and half open ploughland, to be carved out of the richest part of the lovely Calydonian plain. Again and again the old charioteer Oeneus prayed to Meleager. He stood on the threshold of his lofty bedroom and shook the solid wooden doors, imploring his son. Again and again his sisters and his lady mother supplicated him too, though this only made him more obstinate. Again and again his comrades-in-arms tried, the dearest and most cherished friends he had. Even so they could not win him over.

'But then the Curetes began scaling the walls and setting fire to the great town, and the missiles started hailing down on the bedroom itself. At that point, Meleager's well-girdled wife Cleopatra supplicated him in tears. She pictured all the miseries people suffer when their town is captured: they kill the men, fire levels the town, the enemy carry off the children and low-girdled women. Her recital of these disasters touched his heart, and he came out and put on his gleaming armour. In this way, by yielding to his personal feelings, he saved the Aetolians from disaster. But the only result was that his friends gave him none of the many splendid gifts they had earlier offered. He saved them, but got nothing by it.

'Don't, I beg you, think as he did; don't, dear friend, let some god make you follow his example. When the ships are already on fire, it will be all the more difficult to save them. No; come while gifts are still to be had, and the Greeks will treat you like a god. If you plunge into the killing fields with no such gifts, you will not be so respected, even though you turn defeat into victory.'

Swift-footed Achilles replied to him and said:

'Olympian-bred Phoenix, my dear old friend; I have no need of the Greeks' honour. I believe I am honoured because Zeus decrees it so, and this will keep me by my beaked ships as long as breath remains in my body and strength in my limbs.

'And I tell you something else, and you bear it in mind. Don't undermine my resolution with a display of weeping and wailing designed to curry favour with Agamemnon. You must not side with him, or I, who side with you, may come to hate you. Injure the man who injures me – that's your duty, if you're with me; and if you are, then come back and rule my dominions equally with me, share all my privileges.

'These men will report back to the Greeks. Meanwhile, you stay here yourself – there is a soft bed for you to sleep on – and at daybreak we will decide whether to go home or not.'

He spoke, and quietly signalled to Patroclus with a movement of his eyebrows to make up the bed for Phoenix, so that the others might think of getting on their way as soon as possible. Ajax, godlike son of Telamon, now spoke his mind:

'Olympian-born son of Laertes, resourceful Odysseus, let's go. It seems to me our mission is doomed to failure, this time at any rate. Bad as the news is, we must report it at once to the Greeks, who are no doubt sitting up waiting for us. Achilles has hardened his once noble heart and become quite unreasonable – no thought for the affection of us, his comrades, who held him in the highest regard in the whole camp. And so obstinate! After all, even in cases of murder a man accepts a blood-price for the death of a brother or a son. And the killer does not even have to leave his country, if he compensates the next of kin, since that compensation holds the family's anger and injured feelings in check.

'But you, Achilles – the gods have worked you up into this implacable fury over a girl, one, single girl. And here we are, offering you seven of the very best and a great deal more besides. Be gracious. Respect your obligations as our host. We are under your roof, representing the whole Greek army, and we wish for nothing better than to remain your closest and dearest friends among all the Greeks.'

Swift-footed Achilles replied to him and said:

'Olympian-born Ajax, son of Telamon, leader of men, I agree with pretty much everything you seem to be saying. But my heart swells with anger when I think of what happened and the disgraceful way in which Agamemnon treated me in public, like some refugee who counted for nothing.

'Go now and make my decision public. I shall not contemplate bloodshed and warfare again until Hector reaches the huts and ships of my Myrmidons, killing Greeks as he comes, and destroys the ships by fire. However keen to attack he may be, Hector will, I think, be halted when he reaches *my* huts and black ship.'

So he spoke, and each of them took up a two-handled cup, offered a libation and made their way back along the line of ships, with Odysseus at their head.

Patroclus told his men and the waiting-women to make up a comfortable bed for Phoenix as soon as possible. When the women made up the bed as he had ordered with fleeces, a rug and a fine linen sheet, the old man lay down and waited for the coming of divine

Dawn. Achilles himself slept in a corner of his well-built hut with a woman he had brought from Lesbos, fair-cheeked Diomede. Patroclus slept in the corner opposite. He too had a companion, fair-girdled Iphis, whom godlike Achilles had given him after capturing steep Scyros, Enyeus' town.

The envoys reached Agamemnon's huts and were no sooner inside than the Greek lords leapt to their feet, drank to them in welcome from every side with golden cups and bombarded them with questions. Agamemnon lord of men was the first to speak:

'Tell me, celebrated Odysseus, great glory of the Greeks – will he save the ships from being burnt or does he refuse? Is that proud spirit of his still in the grip of his anger?'

All-daring godlike Odysseus replied:

'Most glorious Agamemnon son of Atreus, lord of men, the man has no intention of extinguishing his rage. In fact he is angrier than ever. He rejects you and your gifts. He says you can find out for yourself among the Greeks how to save the ships and men. Meanwhile he threatens to drag his own ships down to the sea at dawn. And he said he advised all the rest of us to sail for home as well: "You are never going to reach your goal in the steep streets of Ilium. Far-thundering Zeus has stretched out a protecting hand over that town, and its people have taken heart." Those were his words.

'Of my fellow envoys, Ajax and the two heralds, both sensible men, are here to bear me out. But the old man Phoenix is sleeping there. Achilles pressed him to stay so that he could embark with him for home in the morning if he wished to, though he said there would be no compulsion.'

So he spoke and was received in complete silence by them all. The bluntness of his words had taken them completely by surprise. For a long time they sat there, speechless and dejected. Eventually Diomedes, master of the battle-cry, spoke out:

'Most glorious Agamemnon son of Atreus, lord of men, you should never have supplicated matchless Achilles and made him such a lavish offer. He is an arrogant man at the best of times, and now you have merely reinforced that arrogance. Well, we'll leave it to him whether he sails or stays. He'll fight again when his heart tells him to, and the god moves him.

'So I suggest we all do what I now propose. For the moment, go to bed – you have satisfied yourselves with the food and wine that a man needs to keep up his strength and courage. When lovely, rosy-fingered Dawn appears, you, Agamemnon, must deploy your infantry and chariots in front of the ships; you must inspire them; and you must fight in the front line yourself.'

So he spoke, and the leaders all shouted their approval, delighted at the words of horse-taming Diomedes. They made their libations and retired to their several huts, where they lay down and took the gift of sleep.

The Death of Patroclus (Book 16)

The Trojans storm the Greek camp, and Achilles sends his dear friend Patroclus to find out what is happening. The wise old Greek advisor Nestor describes the dire situation and begs Patroclus to persuade Achilles at least to allow him (Patroclus) to return to battle.

While this battle was raging round the well-benched ship, Patroclus came up to Achilles shepherd of the people, weeping hot tears like a dark spring trickling black streaks of water down a steep rock-face. Swift-footed godlike Achilles felt pity when he saw him and spoke to him with winged words:

'Patroclus, why are you in tears, like a little girl running along beside her mother and begging to be carried, tugging at her skirt to make her stop, although she is in a hurry, and looking tearfully up at her till at last she picks her up? That, Patroclus, is how you look, with the soft tears rolling down your cheeks. Have you something to tell our Myrmidon troops, or myself? Some news from our home in Phthia that has reached you privately? They say your father Menoetius is still alive, and my father Peleus certainly is, with his Myrmidons around him. If either of them were dead, we should indeed have cause for grief. Or perhaps you are weeping for the Greeks, who are being slaughtered by the hollow ships because of their stupidity? Tell me, don't keep it to yourself. We must share it.'

Sighing heavily, charioteer Patroclus, you replied:

'Achilles son of Peleus, by far the greatest of the Greeks, don't be angry at what I say. It's the Greeks – they are in terrible distress. All our best men are lying by their ships, hit or stabbed. Mighty Diomedes son of Tydeus has been hit; the great spearman Odysseus has been stabbed; so has Agamemnon; and Eurypylus has had an arrow in his thigh. Healers are attending them with all the remedies at their command to try to heal their wounds.

'But you, Achilles, you are impossible. God preserve me from the bitterness you harbour! You and your disastrous greatness – what will future generations have to thank *you* for, if you do nothing to prevent the Greeks' humiliating destruction? You are quite pitiless. Peleus was not your father, or Thetis your mother. No, the grey sea and the sheer cliffs produced you and your unfeeling heart. But if you are privately deterred by some prophecy, some word from Zeus that your lady mother has told you, at least allow *me* to take the field with the Myrmidon contingent at my back, if perhaps I might bring salvation to the Greeks. Give me your own armour to fight in, so that the Trojans take me for you and break off the battle. That would give our weary troops some breathing space – there is little enough respite in war. The Trojans have fought to the point of exhaustion, and I, being fresh, might well drive them back to the town from our ships and huts.'

So Patroclus spoke in supplication, the great fool. In doing so, he was simply invoking his own destiny and a dreadful death. Greatly disturbed, swift-footed Achilles replied:

'Olympian-born Patroclus, what are you talking about? There is no prophecy I know of that I should be paying attention to, and my lady mother has passed on to me no word from Zeus. But it really hurts me when a man who is my equal wants to rob me and take away the prize I won, just because he has more power. After all I have been through in this war, that really hurts me. The army gave me that girl as my prize; I had sacked a walled town; I had won her with my own spear. And now lord Agamemnon son of Atreus snatched her from my arms as if I were some refugee who counted for nothing.

'But that's over and done with: let it go. I was wrong in supposing a man could nurse his anger for ever, though I had intended to do so till the tumult and the fighting reached my own ships. Arm yourself, then, in my famous battle gear and lead my warlike Myrmidons into battle, now that a dark cloud of Trojans is indeed swirling threat-eningly round our ships, and the Greeks are clinging on to a narrow strip of ground with the beach at their back. The whole town has turned out against us, its courage restored.

'No wonder, when they cannot see the helmet on *my* head glinting in their faces. They would soon take to their heels and fill the gullies with their dead, if lord Agamemnon had kindly feelings towards me. As it is, the Greeks are having to defend the very camp itself. Diomedes' spear is no longer raging in his hands to save the Greeks from destruction; and I have not even heard loathsome Agamemnon barking out his orders. It is man-slaying Hector's shouts that ring in my ears, as he hounds on his Trojans. Their cries fill the whole plain: they are trouncing the Greeks.

'Nevertheless, Patroclus, you must save the ships. Attack with all your force before the Trojans send them up in flames and cut us off from home. But listen while I tell you exactly how I want things to be: I want you to win *me* great honour and glory in the eyes of all the Greeks, so that they give my lovely woman back to me and provide splendid gifts as well. So return to me directly you have driven the Trojans from the ships. Even if loud-thundering Zeus offers you the chance of winning glory for yourself, don't entertain any dreams of fighting on without me against these war-loving Trojans. You will diminish my honour.

'So don't lead the Myrmidons on to Ilium in the flush of victory, killing Trojans as you go, or one of the eternal gods from Olympus may cross your path. The Archer-god Apollo loves these Trojans dearly. But turn back when you have lit the way to victory at the ships and leave the rest to do the fighting on the plain. Ah, Father Zeus, Athene and Apollo, if only no Trojan could get away alive, not one, and no Greek either, and we two could survive the massacre to tear off Troy's holy diadem of towers single-handed!'

While Achilles and Patroclus were talking together in this way, the moment came when Ajax could no longer hold his position. He was conquered by the will of Zeus and overwhelmed with spears from the hands of the proud Trojans. His shining helmet, its stout plates struck again and again on both sides, rang terrifyingly about his temples. His left shoulder ached from the prolonged effort of swinging his shield, though even so the volleys of enemy spears were unable to knock it aside. He was panting hard and the sweat streamed from all his limbs. He had no time to catch his breath. Everywhere, disaster piled on disaster.

Tell me now, you Muses that live on Olympus, how the Greek ships were first set on fire! Hector went right up to Ajax, struck Ajax's ash pike with his great sword below the socket of the point and sheared the head clean off. Ajax continued wielding the now headless pike as before, the head finally hitting the ground with a clang a long way below him. Deep in his great heart Ajax realized with a shudder that the gods were taking a hand in the affair and that high-thundering Zeus, intent on a Trojan victory, was thwarting all his battle plans. So he fell back out of range; the Trojans threw blazing brands into the swift ship; and in a moment she was wrapped in inextinguishable flames.

So the fire swirled round her stern. But Achilles slapped his thighs and said to Patroclus:

'Up, Olympian-born Patroclus, charioteer! I can see a blaze of fire roaring up by the ships. They mustn't capture them and cut off our retreat! Quick, get your armour on while I assemble the men.'

So he spoke, and Patroclus armed himself in the gleaming bronze. First he placed fine leg-guards on his shins, fitted with silver ankle-clips. Then he put on Achilles' body-armour, glittering and starry. Over his shoulder he slung his bronze, silver-riveted sword, then his great, heavy shield. On his mighty head he placed his well-made helmet with a horsehair crest, the plume nodding frighteningly from the top. Then he took up two powerful spears that fitted his grip. The only weapon of matchless Achilles he did not take was Achilles' long, thick, heavy spear. No Greek could wield this but Achilles, who alone knew how to handle it. It was made from an ash-tree on the top of Mount Pelion and had been a gift from Cheiron to Achilles' father Peleus, to bring death to warriors.

Patroclus ordered Automedon to yoke the horses at once. He thought more highly of Automedon than of anyone except Achilles breaker of the battle-line, having found that in action he could be completely relied on to keep within calling distance. So Automedon yoked up for him divine Xanthus and Balius, who could race with the winds. Podarge, the storm-filly, had foaled these for their sire the Western Gale when she was grazing in the meadows beside Ocean Stream. Automedon then put in as a trace-horse the thoroughbred Pedasus, whom Achilles had brought away with him when he captured Eëtion's town. Pedasus was only a mortal horse but he could keep up with the immortal pair.

Achilles went the rounds of his huts and got all his Myrmidons under arms. They were like flesh-eating wolves, hearts filled with boundless courage, who have brought down a great antlered stag in the mountains and tear at it, and their jowls run red with blood; then they go off in a pack to lap the black water from the surface of a dark spring with their slender tongues, belching out the gore; their hearts are fearless, and their bellies growl – so the captains and commanders of the Myrmidons surged forward to fall in under the command of Patroclus, Achilles' brave attendant. And there stood warlike Achilles himself, encouraging the charioteers and the shield-bearing infantry.

Each of the fifty swift ships that Achilles had brought to Troy had a crew of fifty men at the oars. He had appointed five commanders whom he trusted to lead them, but he was the most powerful and in overall command. Menesthius of the flashing body-armour had led the first line of ships. He was son of the divine River Spercheus and beautiful Polydora was his mother, a daughter of Peleus. He was thus the child of a woman bedded by a god, the tireless stream Spercheus. But in name he was the son of Borus, because Borus son of Perieres had openly married his mother, giving a handsome dowry.

Warlike Eudorus had commanded the second line. He was the illegitimate son of Polymele daughter of Phylas, a beautiful dancer. The great god Hermes slayer of Argus had fallen for her when he saw her dancing in a chorus for Artemis of the golden distaff, goddess of the hunt. Gracious Hermes took her straight up to her bedroom unobserved, slept with her and made her the mother of this splendid child, Eudorus the great runner and fighter. When the baby had been brought into the light by Eileithyia, the goddess of labour, and saw the rays of the sun, a powerful chieftain, Echecles son of Actor, married the mother after giving an untold

bride-price and took her home with him. So Eudorus'
old grandfather Phylas devotedly raised and looked after
the baby, surrounding him with love as if he were his
own son. Warlike Peisander had commanded the third
line. Of all the Myrmidons he was the best spearman
after Patroclus. The old charioteer Phoenix had led the
fourth and noble Alcimedon the fifth.

When Achilles had drawn them all up, men with
their commanders in their proper ranks, he addressed
them bluntly:

'Myrmidons, let none of you forget what you have
been threatening to do to the Trojans here by the ships
while I indulged my anger. There is not one of you
who did not abuse me: "Obstinate son of Peleus, your
mother suckled you with bile, not milk; you brute,
holding your men back by the ships against their will.
Let's take to our seafaring vessels and sail home again,
since you are in the grip of such pernicious rage." That's
what you said about me when you all got together. Well
now, a bit of real work has come your way, the sort of
fight you have been longing for. So, brave hearts, let the
Trojans have it!'

So he spoke and put fresh heart and courage into
every man, and the ranks closed when they heard their
lord. As a mason fits together blocks of stone when he
builds the wall of a high house to make sure of keep-
ing out the wind, so tightly packed were their helmets
and their bossed shields. They stood so close together,
shield to shield, helmet to helmet, man to man, that
when they moved their heads, the glittering peaks of

59

their plumed helmets met. And in front of them all Patroclus and Automedon stood ready for battle, two men united in their resolution to fight in the forefront of the Myrmidons.

But Achilles went off to his hut, where he lifted the lid of a beautiful inlaid chest which his mother silver-footed Thetis had packed with tunics, wind-proof cloaks and thick rugs, and put on board ship for him to take on his journey. In this he kept a lovely cup, from which he alone drank the sparkling wine and which he himself used for libations to no other god but Father Zeus. He took it from the chest and, after purifying it with sulphur, rinsed it in a lovely stream of water, washed his hands and drew off some sparkling wine. Then, standing in the middle of the forecourt, he prayed and, looking up into the sky, poured out the wine. Zeus who delights in thunder did not fail to notice him:

'Lord Zeus, god of Dodona, god of the Pelasgi, you that live far away and rule over wintry Dodona, sur-rounded by your interpreters the Helloi, who leave their feet unwashed and sleep on the ground; you lis-tened when I prayed to you before and you honoured me by striking a mighty blow at the Greek army. Now grant me another wish. I myself am going to stay here by the ships, but I am sending my comrade with many of my Myrmidons into battle. Grant him victory, far-thundering Zeus, and fill his heart with daring, so that Hector finds out whether my attendant knows how to fight on his own or whether his hands rage invincibly only when *I* throw myself into the grind of battle. And directly he has driven the tumult and the fighting back from the ships, let him come back to me here at my own ships safe and sound with all my armour and close-fighting companions.'

So Achilles spoke in prayer, and Zeus wise in counsel heard him. One half the Father granted, but not the other. The Father agreed that Patroclus should drive the tumult and the fighting back from the ships, but not that he should come back safely from battle. When Achilles had made his libation and prayer to Father Zeus, he went back into his hut and put the cup away in the chest. Then he came out and stood in front of his hut. He still wished to witness the dreadful clash between Trojans and Greeks.

Meanwhile the armed contingents under great-hearted Patroclus advanced and fearlessly attacked the Trojans. They came swarming on like roadside wasps that boys always like to tease, stirring them up in their nest by the road, the young fools: they turn them into a public menace, and if a traveller comes by and unintentionally disturbs them, these brave hearts fly out one and all and protect their little ones – with their courage and spirit the Myrmidons swarmed out in a mass from the ships, and the tumult of battle filled the air. Patroclus then called out to his troops in a loud voice:

'Myrmidons, companions of Achilles, be men, my comrades, call up that fighting spirit of yours and win glory for the son of Peleus, the best man in the Greek camp, with the best warriors under him. Make wide-ruling Agamemnon son of Atreus realize the delusion he is under in giving no respect to the best of all the Greeks.'

So Patroclus spoke and put fresh heart and courage into every man. They fell on the Trojans in a mass and their intimidating roar echoed round the ships.

When the Trojans saw strong Patroclus and his attendant Automedon beside him in all the brilliance of their bronze armour, panic threatened and the ranks began to waver, since they thought swift-footed Achilles must have abandoned his anger and reconciled himself with Agamemnon. Every man looked anxiously around to find some escape from sudden death.

Patroclus was the first to throw a glittering spear. He hurled it straight into the mass of men where the fighting was at its most confused round the stern of Protesilaus' ship and struck Pyraechmes, who had brought his Paeonians in their plumed helmets from Amydon and the broad-flowing River Axius. He hit him in the right shoulder. With a groan Pyraechmes fell on his back in the dust, and his Paeonian troops ran for it. By killing their leader and finest fighter, Patroclus had sown panic among them all. Patroclus, having swept them from the ships, extinguished the fire that was blazing there, leaving the vessel half-burnt. Meanwhile the Trojans fell back with a tremendous din. The Greeks poured forward between the ships, and all hell broke loose.

Like lightning-gatherer Zeus shifting a dense cloud from the high summit of a great mountain, when every lookout place and headland and mountain ravine stands out, and infinite upper air floods down from the skies – so the Greeks saved their ships from going up in flames and for a while could breathe more freely, but they had not done with the fighting. The Trojans had been forced back from the black ships, but not as yet in headlong rout. They still confronted them.

Having broken the Trojan ranks, the Greeks started picking off their men one by one. Brave Patroclus was first to throw his sharp spear at Areilycus and hit him in the thigh just as he had turned. The bronze point drove through and broke the bone; the man fell head-long to the ground. Meanwhile warlike Menelaus struck Thoas in his chest, which he had left exposed above his shield, and brought him down. Amphiclus charged at Meges, but Meges kept his eye on him and got in first with a spear-thrust on the top of the leg where a man's muscle is very thick. The spear-point tore through the tendons, and darkness enveloped Amphiclus' eyes.

Then one of Nestor's sons Antilochus stabbed Atymnius with his sharp spear and drove the bronze head through his side. Atymnius crashed down in front of him. But Maris, infuriated by his brother's death, charged at Antilochus, spear in hand, and planted himself in front of the body. However, before he could do any damage, another son of Nestor, godlike Thrasymedes, made a swift lunge at his shoulder and did not miss. The point of his spear, striking the base of the arm, tore it away from the muscles and completely dislocated the arm-bone. Maris thudded to the ground, and darkness enveloped his eyes. Thus these two men were killed by two brothers and went down to the underworld. Brave spearmen of Sarpedon's contingent, they were the sons of Amisodarus who had reared the Chimaera, the raging monster that brought so many men to grief.

Ajax son of Oïleus dashed into the mêlée where Cleobulus had tripped up and took him alive. But he killed him soon enough with a blow to the neck from his hilted sword, warming the whole blade with blood. Inexorable destiny and purple death closed his eyes. Next, Peneleos and Lycon charged at each other. Each had made a bad throw with his spear and missed the other. So now they ran at one another with their swords. Lycon struck the cone of the other's plumed helmet and his sword broke off at the hilt. But Peneleos slashed Lycon in the neck behind the ear and his sword-blade sliced right through. Nothing held but a piece of skin, and from that Lycon's head dangled down as he sank to the ground.

Meriones, too fast for Acamas, caught him up and stabbed him in the right shoulder as he was about to mount his chariot. Acamas crashed out of the chariot and a mist descended on his eyes. Meanwhile, Idomeneus struck Erymas on the mouth with his relentless bronze. The metal point of the spear penetrated under his brain and smashed the white jaw-bones. His teeth were knocked out; both his eyes filled with blood; and gasping for breath, he blew blood through his mouth and nostrils. Death's black cloud enveloped him.

So each of these Greek chieftains killed his man. Just as predatory wolves harry lambs or kids and snatch them away from their mothers when they have become separated on the mountains through the shepherd's carelessness, and the wolves seize their chance to pick off the timid creatures – so the Greeks harried the Trojans. The Trojans could think only of tumultuous retreat, and all the fight went out of them.

It was now the one desire of great Ajax son of Telamon to hit bronze-clad Hector with his spear. But Hector was no inexperienced fighter. He protected his broad shoulders with his bull's hide shield, and his ear was alert to the whistle of arrows and thud of spears. He was well aware that the enemy's reinforcements had won them the day, but even so he held his position and tried to save his loyal men.

As Zeus unleashes a tempest after clear weather, driving storm-clouds into the skies from Olympus, so the Trojans started yelling and panicking, and they fled across the Greeks' defensive ditch in no semblance of order. Hector's speedy horses carried him off, arms and all, and he left to their fate the men who had become unintentionally ensnared by the ditch. For many a pair of swift war-horses snapped off their shafts at the yoke as they tried to climb the ditch, leaving their master's chariot behind.

Patroclus chased them with slaughter in his heart, urging on the Greeks relentlessly, while yelling, panicking Trojans, now separated from each other, filled every track. Swirls of dust went rolling up to the clouds as their strong horses made at full speed for the town, leaving the Greek ships and their huts behind them. Wherever Patroclus saw the greatest numbers of chariots in wild retreat, there he followed up, yelling threats. Men tumbled headlong from their chariots beneath his axles, and their chariots flipped over. But Patroclus' immortal swift horses, the splendid gift given by the gods to Achilles' father Peleus, pressed on without a check and cleared the ditch at a single bound. It was Hector he was after, Hector he yearned to kill. But Hector's swift horses carried him to safety.

As in autumn the whole countryside grows dark and heavy with rain under a stormy sky when Zeus sends torrential downpours; he is angry, and rages at men who deliver crooked rulings in public assembly and drive justice out, regardless of the eye of the gods. All the streams run in spate, torrents scar the terraced hillsides, and rivers rush headlong down from the mountains with a great roar into the turbid sea, washing away the fields – such was the din that went up from the Trojan chariots as they fled.

Patroclus had by now cut off the nearest Trojan contingents and was herding them back towards the ships. He defeated all their efforts to get back to Ilium and there, between the ships, the river and the high wall, he kept charging in and killing men, exacting the penalty for so many Greek dead. First he threw his shining spear at Pronous and hit him on the chest which he had left exposed above his shield: this brought him down, and he thudded to the ground. Next he attacked Thestor, who was sitting hunched up in his polished chariot. This man had lost his senses, and the reins had slipped from his hands. Patroclus came up beside him and stabbed him on the right side of the jaw, driving the spear between his teeth. Then, using the spear as a lever, he hoisted him over the chariot-rail, as a fisherman sitting on a jutting rock pulls a lively fish out of the sea with his line and shining hook. So with his bright spear Patroclus hauled his gaping catch out of the chariot and dropped him on his face to die where he fell. Next, as Erylaus rushed at him, he hit him with a rock full on the head. Inside the heavy helmet the man's skull was split in two; he fell face downward on the ground, and heart-crushing death engulfed him. Then Patroclus dealt with Erymas, Amphoterus and Epaltes; Tlepolemus, Echius and Pyris; Ipheus, Euippus and Polymelus, bringing them down in swift succession to the bountiful earth.

When Sarpedon saw how his beltless Lycians were falling to Patroclus son of Menoetius, he turned on his godlike warriors:

'Shame on you, Lycians! Where are you off to? Come on, now! I'm going to take on that man over there. I intend to find out who it is that's carrying all before him and has done the Trojans so much harm already, bringing down so many of our best men.'

He spoke and, fully armed, leapt from his chariot to the ground, and on the other side Patroclus, when he saw him, did the same. As two vultures with their crooked claws and curved beaks fight on a rocky height and scream as they fight, so the two men, uttering defiant cries, made for each other.

Zeus, son of sickle-wielding Cronus, saw what was happening and took pity on them. Then he spoke to Hera, his sister and wife:

'This is an unhappy business! My son Sarpedon,

dearest of men, is destined to be killed by Patroclus son of Menoetius. I wonder now – I am in two minds. Shall I snatch him up and set him down alive on Lycia's rich soil, far from the war with all its tears? Or shall I now let him fall at Patroclus' hands?'

Ox-eyed lady Hera replied:

'Dread son of Cronus, what are you suggesting now? Are you proposing to reprieve from the pains of death a mortal man whose destiny has long been settled? Do what you like, then; but not all the rest of us gods will approve.

'But I will tell you something else, and you bear it in mind. If you send Sarpedon home alive, consider whether some other god might not want to do the same for a son of his in the heat of battle. Many of those fighting it out round Troy are the sons of gods who would resent your action bitterly. If Sarpedon is dear to you and your heart grieves for him, let him fall in the thick of the action against Patroclus and, when the breath of life has left him, send Death and sweet Sleep to take him up and bring him to the broad realm of Lycia, where his relatives and retainers will give him burial with a grave-mound and monument, the honour that is due to the dead.'

So she spoke, and the Father of men and gods complied. But he did send down a shower of bloody raindrops to the earth in tribute to his dear son whom Patroclus was about to kill in fertile Troy, far from the land of his fathers.

When the two had come within range of each other,

Patroclus threw. He hit famous Thrasydemus, lord Sarpedon's fine attendant, in the lower belly and brought him down. Sarpedon, throwing second with his shining spear, missed Patroclus but struck his horse Pedasus on the right shoulder. The horse keeled over, gasping for breath, fell whinnying in the dust, and its life departed. The other two horses sprang apart; the yoke creaked under the strain; and their reins became entangled, since their trace-horse lay in the dust. But the great spearman Automedon soon found the remedy. He drew the long sword from his sturdy thigh, jumped down and deftly cut the trace-horse clear. The pair straightened themselves up and were pulled in by the reins, and the two men resumed their soul-destroying duel.

Sarpedon then missed with a glittering spear; the point passed harmlessly over Patroclus' left shoulder and failed to make its mark. But Patroclus threw his spear, and the weapon did not leave his hand for nothing. It struck Sarpedon where the lungs enclosed his dense heart, and he crashed down as an oak crashes down or a poplar or a towering pine which woodsmen cut down in the mountains with their newly sharpened axes to make timbers for a ship. So Sarpedon lay stretched in front of his chariot and horses, gurgling and clutching at the bloodstained dust. As a lion gets in among a herd and kills a proud tawny bull among the shambling cows, and the bull, dying under the lion's jaws, bellows – so Sarpedon, leader of the shield-bearing Lycians, struggled defiantly to speak as he yielded up his life to Patroclus, and called on his dear companion:

'Glaucus, old friend, champion among men, now's the time to show your bravery and ability as a fighter. Now make deadly war your one desire, if you have it in you. Run to our Lycian leaders everywhere and urge them on to rally round Sarpedon. Then fight over me with your own spear. Every day of your life you will bear the blame and disgrace if you let the Greeks strip me of my arms, here where I fell beside their ships. Hold firm, then, with all your strength and throw every man we have into the fight.'

As Sarpedon spoke, the end that is death enveloped his eyes and cut short his breath. Patroclus put his foot on his chest and withdrew the spear from his flesh. The innards came with it: he had drawn out the spear-point and the man's life together. Close by, the Myrmidons held on to Sarpedon's snorting horses, who were ready to bolt now they had left their masters' chariot.

Glaucus was distraught when he heard Sarpedon's call. His inability to help him wrung his heart; and he gripped his damaged arm with his good hand, hurting as he was from the arrow-wound that Teucer, defending his companions, had given him when he charged at the high Greek wall. Then he prayed to the Archer-god Apollo:

'Listen to me, lord, you who are somewhere in the rich land of Lycia or in Troy; wherever you are, you can hear a man in distress, as I am now. I've received this cruel wound. The pain driving through my arm is excruciating; the blood refuses to dry up; my shoulder's paralysed; I can't hold my spear steady or go out and fight the enemy. And now our best man has been killed,

Sarpedon son of Zeus. But Zeus will not lift a finger, even for his own son. But you, lord Apollo, heal this cruel wound, soothe away the pain and give me strength to call on the Lycians and urge them into battle, while I fight over the body of the dead man myself.'

So he spoke in prayer, and Phoebus Apollo heard him and at once relieved the pain, dried up the dark blood from the ugly wound and filled him with fresh energy. Glaucus realized what had happened and rejoiced that the great god had responded so quickly to his prayer. He went at once to all the Lycian leaders everywhere and urged them to rally round Sarpedon. Then he went striding off to find some Trojans also, Polydamas and godlike Agenor, Aeneas and bronze-armoured Hector. He went up to them and spoke winged words:

'Hector, you have completely forgotten your allies, who are giving their lives for you far from their dear ones and the land of their fathers. You show no eagerness to help them. Sarpedon, leader of the shield-bearing Lycians, lies dead. He was the upright and strong defender of the Lycian realm, and now the bronze-clad War-god Ares has cut him down under Patroclus' spear. Make a stand by him, my friends. Think of the shame of it, if the Myrmidons, angry for the many Greeks who fell to our spears beside their swift ships, should take Sarpedon's arms and desecrate his body.'

So he spoke, and the Trojans could not contain their overwhelming, inconsolable grief, since Sarpedon, though a foreigner, had been a mainstay of their town and the finest warrior among the many he had brought with him. Eager to avenge him, they made straight for the Greeks with Hector in the forefront, infuriated by Sarpedon's death.

Meanwhile manly Patroclus spurred on the Greeks. First he spoke to the Ajaxes, both already intent on combat:

'You two Ajaxes, now make it your mission to fight off the enemy like the men you have always been, or even better. Sarpedon lies dead. He was the first man to storm the Greek wall. Let's see if we can capture and mangle his body, strip the armour from his back and at the same time slaughter some of the friends who will protect him.'

So he spoke, and they were already spoiling for the fight. And now, when the two forces, Trojans and Lycians on the one side, Greeks and Myrmidons on the other, had strengthened their ranks, they joined battle over the fallen Sarpedon with terrifying cries. The armour on men's bodies rang aloud, and Zeus eclipsed the field of battle in dreadful night to make the struggle over his dear son all the more murderous.

At first the Trojans were able to repel the dark-eyed Greeks, who lost one of the best men in the Myrmidon force, godlike Epeigeus. He had at one time been ruler of prosperous Budeion but, having killed a brave relative, he took sanctuary with Peleus and his wife silver-footed Thetis, who sent him to Ilium land of horses in the company of Achilles, breaker of men, to fight the Trojans. Epeigeus had just laid his hands on Sarpedon's body when glorious Hector hurled a rock which struck him on the head. Inside the heavy helmet his skull was split in two; he fell face down across the body, and heart-crushing death engulfed him.

Patroclus, distressed at his comrade's loss, raced through the front line like a swift falcon when it scatters the jackdaws and the starlings. That was how you, charioteer Patroclus, flew at the Lycians and Trojans, in fury at the death of your friend. Patroclus threw a boulder at the neck of Sthenelaus and smashed the tendons. The Trojan front line and glorious Hector himself fell back before his onslaught. As far as a man throws a long, light spear when he is doing his best in the games or in battle against an enemy thirsting for his blood, so far did the Trojans withdraw and the Greeks press forward.

Glaucus, leader of the shield-bearing Lycians, was the first to halt. He turned and killed great-hearted Bathycles, who lived in Hellas and stood out as one of the most prosperous of the Myrmidons. Bathycles was about to catch him up when Glaucus suddenly turned on his pursuer and stabbed him with his spear in the middle of the chest. He thudded to the ground. The loss of this brave man was a heavy blow to the Greeks; but the Trojans were delighted and massed in numbers round Glaucus.

The Greeks, however, had lost none of their fight and still bore energetically down on the enemy. It was now the turn of Meriones to kill a Trojan man-at-arms, daring Laogonus who was priest of Idaean Zeus and was honoured by the people like a god. Meriones struck him under the jaw and ear. Life swiftly left his limbs, and hateful darkness engulfed him.

Aeneas then hurled a spear at Meriones, hoping

to catch him as he strode forward under cover of his shield. But Meriones was on the lookout and avoided the bronze spear. He ducked under it, and the long shaft stuck in the ground behind him, its butt-end quivering till the imperious War-god Ares took away its force. Aeneas was enraged and said:

'Meriones, you may be a fine dancer, but my spear would have stopped you for good and all, if only I'd hit you.'

The famous spearman Meriones said:

'Aeneas, powerful though you are, it would be difficult for you to extinguish the fire of everyone you met in action. You are made of mortal stuff like the rest of us, and if I caught you in the belly with a sharp spear, you would, for all your strength and confidence, immediately yield the glory to me and your life to the god Hades, famed for his horses.'

So he spoke, and Patroclus, brave son of Menoetius, reproved him:

'Meriones, you're too fine a warrior to spend your time making speeches. Believe me, old friend, the Trojans are not going to be pushed back from Sarpedon's body by a few insults; the earth will cover many a man first. Battles are won by deeds; the council-chamber is the place for words. This is no time to talk, but to fight.'

With these words he led the way and godlike Meriones went with him. Like the crashing that rises from woodcutters at work in a mountain glade, and the noise is heard a long way off, so from the broad earth there rose the thud of bronze, leather and well-made shields as men stabbed at each other with swords and curved spears. Even the sharpest eye would never have recognized godlike Sarpedon, enveloped as he was from head to foot in weapons, blood and dust. Men swarmed round his body as flies in a sheepfold buzz round the brimming pails in spring-time when the vessels overflow with milk.

So they swarmed round the body and, as they did so, Zeus never shifted his shining eyes from the thick of battle but kept them always fixed on the men, thinking to himself about the killing of Patroclus. He was in two minds whether to let him fall to glorious Hector's spear in the thick of the action over godlike Sarpedon and let Hector strip the armour from his shoulders, or whether to allow Patroclus to bring still more of his enemies to grief. In the end Zeus decided the best thing was for Patroclus, Achilles' fine attendant, to drive the Trojans and bronze-armoured Hector back towards the town, taking many lives.

So Zeus made a coward of Hector. He leapt into his chariot and wheeled it round for flight, shouting to the other Trojans to take to their heels – he knew Zeus had tipped the sacred scales against him. At that, not even the mighty Lycians stood their ground; they fled one and all. They had seen their own lord hit in the heart and lying where the dead were heaped. For in the fierce conflict Zeus had staged, many a man had been killed over Sarpedon's body.

So the Greeks stripped the gleaming bronze armour from Sarpedon's shoulders. Brave Patroclus son of Menoetius handed it to his men and told them to take it to the hollow ships. Then Zeus who marshals the clouds addressed Apollo:

'Quick, dear Phoebus, go and take Sarpedon out of range and, when you have wiped the dark blood off, carry him to some distant spot and wash him in running water, anoint him with ambrosia and wrap him in an immortal robe. Then send him to be borne away by Sleep and his twin-brother Death, those swift attendants, who will quickly set him down in broad Lycia's fertile realm where his relatives and retainers will give him burial with a grave-mound and monument – the honour that is due to the dead.'

So he spoke, and Apollo did not turn a deaf ear, but descended from the mountains of Ida into the mayhem of the fight. At once he took godlike Sarpedon out of range and, carrying him to some distant spot, washed him in running water, anointed him with ambrosia and wrapped him in an immortal robe. Then he sent him to be borne away by Sleep and his twin-brother Death, those swift attendants, who quickly set him down in broad Lycia's fertile realm.

Patroclus, with a shout to his charioteer Automedon, went in pursuit of the Trojans and Lycians. He was completely deluded, the blind fool. Had he kept to his orders from Achilles, he would have saved himself from the evil destiny which is dark death. But the will of Zeus always prevails over men. Zeus can easily make a brave man run away and lose a battle, but at another time that very same god will urge him on to fight. Now he put heart into Patroclus.

Who was the first man, who the last, to fall to you, Patroclus, as the gods summoned you to your death? Adrestus first, and Autonous and Echeclus; Perimus, Epistor and Melanippus; and then Elasus and Mulius and Pylartes. All these Patroclus killed, though the rest of them had had the sense to run. He was raging so unstoppably with his spear that the Trojans' city with its high gates would now have fallen to the Greeks under Patroclus if Phoebus Apollo had not taken his stand on the well-built tower with death in mind for Patroclus and salvation for the Trojans. Three times Patroclus scaled an angle of the high wall and three times Apollo hurled him off, thrusting back his glittering shield with his immortal hands. But when he came on like something superhuman for the fourth time, the god gave a terrible shout and spoke winged words:

'Back, Olympian-born Patroclus! The town of the proud Trojans is not destined to be captured by your spear nor even by Achilles, who is a far better man than you.'

So he spoke, and Patroclus retreated a good way back to avoid the wrath of the Archer-god Apollo.

Hector had pulled up his horses at the Scaean gate. There he debated whether to drive into the mêlée once more and fight, or to order all his men to withdraw into the town. He was still in two minds when Phoebus Apollo appeared beside him, resembling vigorous and powerful Asius, horse-taming Hector's uncle (Asius was a brother of Hecabe and a son of Dymas who lived in Phrygia on the banks of the River Sangarius). In this disguise Apollo son of Zeus said:

'Hector, why have you stopped fighting and neglected your duty? I wish I were as much your better as you are mine! Then you would soon regret your withdrawal from battle. Off with you now and set your powerful horses at Patroclus. You could catch him yet, and Apollo grant you the victory.'

With these words the god went back into the battling crowd, and glorious Hector told warlike Cebriones to lash his horses into the fight. Apollo, merging with the throng, created terrible mayhem among the Greeks and gave the upper hand to Hector and the Trojans. But Hector ignored the rest of the Greeks and, killing none of them, drove his powerful horses straight at Patroclus. Patroclus on his side leapt from his chariot to the ground with his spear in his left hand.

With the other he picked up a jagged, sparkling stone – his hand just covered it – and, refusing to retreat before Hector, threw it with all his force. He did not throw in vain: the sharp stone caught Hector's charioteer Cebriones, famous Priam's illegitimate son, on the forehead, with the horses' reins still in his hands. It shattered both his eyebrows, crushing the bone; and his eyes fell out and rolled in the dust at his feet. He fell back out of the well-built chariot like a diver, and life left his bones. Mocking him, charioteer Patroclus, you said:

'Well, well! How light on his toes, judging by that acrobatic somersault! Now, if the delightful dive he has taken from the chariot on to the plain is anything to go by, he'd satisfy the hunger of lots of people by doing the same at sea. Even in the roughest weather he could leap off a boat and grope about for molluscs. I never knew the Trojans had such acrobats!'

With these words he advanced to claim the body of the warrior Cebriones, springing like a lion that has been wounded in the chest while assaulting the folds, and his courage is the death of him. With such determination, Patroclus, did you hurl yourself at Cebriones.

Hector on the other side leapt from his chariot to the ground, and the two fought for Cebriones like a pair of lions on the mountain heights, each as hungry and fearless as the other, disputing the dead body of a stag. So, with the body of Cebriones between them, these two champions of the battle-cry, Patroclus and glorious Hector, longed to hack into each other's flesh with their cruel spears. Hector got hold of Cebriones' head and never once let go; Patroclus, at his end, clung to a foot; and the rest of the Trojans and Greeks joined in the fierce confrontation.

Like the east and south winds tussling with one another in a mountain glen, setting the dense wood heaving, beech and ash and smooth-barked cornel: their long boughs lash each other with a terrifying sound, and the branches snap noisily – so the Trojans and Greeks leapt at one another and destroyed. There was no thought of fatal flight on either side. The ground where Cebriones fell was peppered with sharp spears and feathered arrows that had leapt from the bowstring; huge rocks struck shields and sent staggering those that fought about him. And there great Cebriones lay, in a swirl of dust, great even in his fall, his charioteering days forgotten.

While the sun was high in the sky, volley and counter-volley found their mark and men kept falling. But when the sun began to drop – towards the time when the ploughman unyokes his ox – the Greeks got the upper hand in defiance of destiny. They dragged the warrior Cebriones out from among the weapons and the yelling Trojans, and stripped the armour from his back.

But Patroclus, with murder in his heart, leapt on the enemy. Three times he charged with an intimidating yell, like impetuous Ares, and three times he killed nine men. But when he leapt in like something superhuman for the fourth time, then, Patroclus, the end was in sight. In the heat of the battle, Phoebus encountered you, Phoebus most terrible.

Patroclus had not seen him coming through the mayhem; the god had wrapped himself in a thick mist for this meeting. He stood behind Patroclus now and, striking his back and broad shoulders with the flat of his hand, he made Patroclus' eyes spin and knocked the helmet off his head. With its heavy vizor it rolled clattering away under the horses' hooves, and its plume was defiled with blood and dust. It had not been allowed to defile that crested helmet in the dust before, when it protected the head and handsome face of godlike Achilles. But now Zeus granted it to Hector to wear, since he was very close to death. The long-shadowed spear, huge, thick and heavy with its head of bronze, was shattered in Patroclus' hands. The fringed shield with its strap fell from his shoulder to the ground; and lord Apollo son of Zeus undid the body-armour on his chest.

A fatal blindness overtook Patroclus. His shining limbs were paralysed; and as he stood there in a daze, a Dardanian called Euphorbus, son of Panthous, came up behind him at close range, threw a sharp spear and hit him in the middle of the back between the shoulders. This Euphorbus was the best spearman, runner and horseman of his years and in this very battle (the first he had fought as a charioteer learning the art of war) he had already brought twenty men from their chariots to the ground. He was the first, then, to let fly at you, charioteer Patroclus. But he did not kill you. After pulling out the ash spear from his flesh, he ran back and mingled with the crowd. He did not stay to fight Patroclus, defenceless though he was.

And now, overcome by the god's blow and Euphorbus' spear, Patroclus began to retreat into his own contingent of warriors to avoid death. When Hector saw great-hearted Patroclus wounded and in retreat, he made his way towards him through the ranks and, coming up, stabbed him with his spear in the lower belly, driving the bronze clean through. Patroclus thudded to the ground, throwing the whole Greek army into consternation. As a lion's will to fight overpowers an indomitable wild boar when the fearless pair battle it out in the mountains over a little stream; both wish to drink there, but the lion's strength prevails and his panting enemy is overcome – so, after killing many men himself, Menoetius' strong son fell to a close-range thrust from Hector, who now spoke to him in triumph with winged words:

'Patroclus, you probably thought you'd sack our town,

make Trojan women slaves and ship them off to the land of your fathers. You innocent! In their defence, Hector's swift horses were racing into battle – I, Hector, finest spearman of the war-loving Trojans, who stand between them and the day of slavery. As for you, vultures are going to eat you on this very spot. Miserable wretch! Even great Achilles did not save you. I can imagine all the instructions he gave you on your way out, while he stayed behind: "Charioteer Patroclus, don't come back to the hollow ships till you have ripped through the tunic on man-slaying Hector's chest and soaked it with his blood." That, I imagine, is what he must have said; and like an idiot you took him at his word.'

Fading fast you replied, charioteer Patroclus:

'Hector, boast loud and long while you can. Zeus and Apollo handed you that victory. *They* conquered me. It was an easy task: they took the armour from my back. If twenty men like you had confronted me, they would all have fallen to my spear. No: it was deadly destiny and Leto's son Apollo that did for me. Then came a man, Euphorbus; you are the third of them all to kill me. But I will tell you something else, and you bear it in mind. You too, I swear it, have not long to live. Already you stand in the shadow of death and inexorable destiny, slaughtered at the hands of Achilles, the matchless son of Peleus.'

As he spoke, the end that is death enveloped him. Life left his limbs and took wing for the house of Hades, bewailing its lot and the youth and the manhood it had left behind. But glorious Hector spoke to him again, though he was gone:

'Patroclus, why prophesy an early end for me? Who knows – Achilles, son of lovely-haired Thetis, may still get there first, dispatched with a blow from my spear.'

With these words Hector put his foot on Patroclus to withdraw his bronze spear from the wound, and trod the body off it to lie face upwards on the ground. Then without a pause he went after Automedon, Achilles' godlike attendant, with his spear. He was eager to hit him. But Automedon was carried out of harm's way by his speedy immortal horses, the splendid gift that Peleus had received from the gods.

Achilles' Decision (Book 18)

Patroclus' body is saved, but the armour which he is wearing is seized by Hector.

So they fought on like blazing fire. Meanwhile Antilochus, swift-footed messenger, came to Achilles with his news and found him in front of his beaked ships. Achilles harboured a premonition of what had already happened and, disturbed, was reflecting on the situation:

'What's going on? Why are the long-haired Greeks stampeding wildly for their ships across the plain? I pray the gods have not brought about the grief and suffering my mother once predicted for me. She told me that, while I was still alive, the best of the Myrmidons would fall to the Trojans and leave the light of day. And now I am sure Menoetius' brave son Patroclus is dead. The hothead! I ordered him to come back here when he'd saved the ships from the flames and not fight it out with Hector.'

While these thoughts raced through his mind, noble Antilochus, Nestor's son, halted before him, hot tears pouring down his cheeks, and gave him the agonizing news:

'What can I say, son of warlike Peleus? You are about to hear dreadful news. If only it weren't true. Patroclus lies dead. They are fighting over his body. It's been stripped. Hector of the flashing helmet has your armour.'

So he spoke, and a black cloud of grief engulfed Achilles. He picked up the sooty dust in both his hands and poured it over his head. He begrimed his handsome features with it, and black ashes settled on his sweet-smelling tunic. Great Achilles lay spread out in the dust, a giant of a man, clawing at his hair with his hands and mangling it. The female slaves he and Patroclus had captured shrieked aloud and in their grief ran out of doors to surround warlike Achilles. They beat their breasts with their hands and sank to the ground. On the other side Antilochus, shedding tears of misery, gripped Achilles' hands. Achilles was sobbing out his noble heart, and Antilochus was afraid he might take a knife and cut his throat.

Achilles let out an intimidating cry, and his lady mother heard him where she sat in the depths of the sea beside her ancient father. Then she herself took up the cry of grief, and there gathered round her every goddess, every Nereid that was in the deep salt sea. Glauce was there and Thaleia and Cymodoce; Nesaea, Speio, Thoe and ox-eyed Halie; Cymothoe, Actaee and Limnoreia; Melite, Iaera, Amphithoe and Agaue; Doto, Proto too, Pherusa and Dynamene; Dexamene, Amphinome and Callianeira; Doris and Panope and famous, far-sung Galatea; Nemertes and Apseudes and Callianassa; Clymene came too, with Ianeira, Ianassa, Maera, Oreithuia, lovely-haired Amatheia, and other Nereids of the salt-sea depths. The silvery cave was full of Nymphs. With one accord they beat their breasts, and Thetis led them in their lamentations:

'Listen to me, my sister Nereids, and know the sorrows of my heart. How wretched I am, unhappy mother of the best of men! I brought into the world a matchless son, a mighty man, greatest of warriors. I nursed him as one tends a little plant in a garden bed and he shot up like a sapling. I sent him to Ilium in his ships to fight against the Trojans; and never again now shall I welcome him home to Peleus' house. And yet he has to suffer, every day he lives and sees the sun; and I can do no good by going to his side. But I *will* go, none the less, to see my dear child and hear what anguish has come to him in his absence from the fighting.'

With these words she left the cave. The rest went with her, weeping, and on either side of them the surging sea fell back. When they reached fertile Troy, they came up one by one on to the beach where the Myrmidon ships had been drawn up on the shore round swift Achilles. His lady mother went up to him as he lay groaning there and with a piercing cry took her son's head in her hands and lamenting spoke winged words:

'My child, why these tears? Why this sorrow? Tell me, don't keep it to yourself. What you prayed for when you lifted up your hands to Zeus has been fulfilled by him: the Greeks have been penned in at the ships because of your absence and suffered the ugly consequences.'

Swift-footed Achilles sighed heavily and said:

'Mother, the Olympian has indeed done what I asked. But what satisfaction can I get from that, now that my dearest companion is dead, Patroclus, who was more to me than any other of my men, whom I loved as much as my own life? I have destroyed Patroclus. And Hector who killed him has stripped him of my armour, my awe-inspiring, wonderful, magnificent armour that the gods gave as a splendid gift to Peleus on the day they brought you to the bed of a mortal man in marriage. How I wish you had stayed there with the deathless salt-sea Nymphs, and Peleus had taken home a mortal wife! But as it is, you became my mother; and now, to multiply *your* sorrows too, you are going to lose your son and never welcome him home again. For I have no wish to live and linger in the world of men, unless, before all else, Hector is hit by my spear and dies, paying the price for slaughtering Patroclus son of Menoetius.'

Thetis said in tears:

'If that is so, my child, you do not have long to live; you are doomed to die immediately after Hector –'

Deeply disturbed, swift-footed Achilles replied:

'Then let me die immediately, since I let my companion be killed when I could have saved him. He has fallen, far from the land of his fathers, needing my help to defend him from death. But now, since I shall never see the land of my fathers again, since I have proved no defence for Patroclus or for all my many other comrades whom god-like Hector killed, but have sat here by my ships, an idle burden on the earth, a man who fights like no other in all the Greek army, though others are better in debate . . . ah, how I wish rivalry could be banished from the world of gods and men, and with it anger, which makes the wisest man flare up and spreads much sweeter than dripping honey through his whole being, like smoke – anger such as lord Agamemnon has now provoked in me!

'But however much it still rankles, it is now over and done with: let it go. We must master our pride. We have no choice. So now I will go and seek out Hector, the destroyer of that dear life. As for my death, when Zeus and the other immortal gods appoint it, I will welcome it. Even mighty Heracles could not escape his doom, dear as he was to lord Zeus son of Cronus, but was laid low by destiny and Hera's bitter anger. So I too shall lie low in death, if the same destiny awaits me.

'But now, may I win heroic glory! I will make these Trojan women and full-girdled daughters of Dardanus wipe the tears from their tender cheeks with both their hands as they raise the funeral dirge, to teach them that I have been away from battle too long. And you, Mother, as you love me, don't keep me from battle. You will never persuade me now.'

The goddess silver-footed Thetis replied:

'Indeed, my child, it would be no bad thing for you to save your exhausted comrades from the death that stares them in the face. But your fine, sparkling bronze armour is in Trojan hands. Hector of the flashing helmet is swaggering about in it himself – not, I think, that he will glory in it long, for he is very near death. So don't throw yourself into the grind of battle till you see me here again. I shall come back at sunrise tomorrow with a fine set of armour from lord Hephaestus.'

With these words she turned away from her son and spoke to her sister Nereids:

'Plunge now into the broad bosom of the deep and make your way to the Old Man of the Sea and our father's house. Tell him everything. I myself am going to high Olympus to ask the famous blacksmith Hephaestus whether he would like to give my son an impressive set of shining armour.'

So she spoke, and the Nymphs now disappeared from view into the waves of the sea, and the goddess silver-footed Thetis set out for Olympus to fetch an impressive set of armour for her dear son.

While she was on her way to Olympus, the Greek men-at-arms, escaping with cries of terror from manslaying Hector, streamed back to the ships and the Hellespont. It was almost more than they could do to drag the body of Achilles' attendant Patroclus out of range of the missiles. The Trojan infantry and chariots and Hector, like fire in his courage, caught up with it again. Three times glorious Hector, coming up behind and shouting for his men's support, seized it by the feet and tried to drag it back; three times the two Ajaxes, clothed in martial valour, flung him back from the body.

But Hector's resolution was unshaken. When he was not hurling himself into the mêlée, he stood his ground, shouting his great battle-cry, and he never once fell back. As shepherds in the fields are unable to chase a famished tawny lion off its kill, so the bronze-armoured Ajaxes could not chase Priam's son Hector away from the body. In fact Hector would have hauled it away and won unutterable glory, if swift Iris, quick as the wind, had not come running down from Olympus to tell Achilles to prepare for battle. Hera sent her without telling Zeus and the other gods. Coming up to Achilles she spoke winged words:

'Up, son of Peleus, most impetuous of men – rise and defend Patroclus! They're fighting tooth and nail for him, and men are killing men beside the ships, the Greeks in their efforts to protect his body, the Trojans in the hope of hauling it away to windswept Ilium. Glorious Hector above all is determined to drag off Patroclus. He wants to cut his head from his soft neck and stick it on the palisade. So get up! Stop lying there! You should feel ashamed that Patroclus might become the plaything of the dogs of Ilium. It's you who'll be disgraced if he goes mutilated to the dead below.'

Swift-footed godlike Achilles replied:

'Divine Iris, which of the gods sent you to me with this message?'

Swift Iris, quick as the wind, replied:

'It was Hera, honourable wife of Zeus, that sent me. The son of Cronus who sits on high was not told, nor was any other of the gods that live on snowy Olympus.'

Swift-footed Achilles replied and said:

'But how can I go into action? They've got my armour, and my own mother has forbidden me to prepare for battle till I see her back here. She promised to bring me fine arms from Hephaestus. I don't know of anyone else whose armour I could wear, except maybe the shield of Ajax son of Telamon. But he, I expect, will be in his place in the front line, causing havoc with his spear for the dead Patroclus.'

Swift Iris, quick as the wind, replied:

'We gods are well aware your famous armour has been taken. But go to the ditch anyway, as you are, and show yourself to the Trojans. They may be unnerved by you and break off the battle. That would give your weary troops some breathing space – there is little enough respite in war.'

With these words swift-footed Iris took her leave, and Achilles dear to Zeus rose up. Athene threw her fringed aegis round his mighty shoulders and the celestial goddess also crowned him with a golden cloud around his head, and from it a blaze of light shone out. Just as smoke goes up to the skies from a town on some far-away beleaguered island which enemy troops are besieging: all day long the men fight a desperate battle from their town walls, but at sunset beacon-fires blaze up one after the other, and the light shoots up into the sky for neighbours to see and come to the rescue in their ships – so the gleam from Achilles' head reached the skies.

He went beyond the wall and took his stand by the ditch; but, remembering his mother's careful instructions, did not join the Greeks in battle. There he stood and gave a shout, while in the distance Pallas Athene raised the war-cry too. This threw the Trojans into unutterable chaos. Like the piercing sound that rings out from a trumpet when a town is surrounded by murderous enemies, such was Achilles' piercing cry. The Trojans heard his bronze voice, and panic threatened. Even the lovely-maned horses sensed death in the air and began to pull their chariots round. Their charioteers were dumbfounded as they saw the inexhaustible fire, fed by the goddess grey-eyed Athene, blaze fearfully from the head of great-hearted Achilles son of Peleus.

Three times godlike Achilles sent his voice ringing out over the ditch, three times the Trojans and their famous allies were thrown into chaos. Twelve of their best men perished then and there, entangled among their own chariots and spears.

Meanwhile, with thankful hearts the Greeks pulled Patroclus out of range. They laid him on a bier and his dear companions gathered round him, weeping. Swift-footed Achilles accompanied them, and the hot tears poured down his cheeks when he saw his faithful companion lying on the bier pierced by the sharp bronze spear. He had sent him into battle with his chariot and horses, never to welcome him home on his return.

Ox-eyed lady Hera now told the tireless sun to return, unwillingly, into the Stream of Ocean. The sun set, and the godlike Greeks enjoyed a respite from the fierce struggle and war, the great leveller.

The Trojans on their side withdrew from the heat of battle, unyoked the swift horses from their chariots and, before thinking of food, gathered together to assess the situation. Nobody dared sit down, and they held the meeting on their feet, since all of them had been appalled by Achilles' reappearance after his long absence from war and its agonies. The discussion was begun by wise Polydamas, the only man among them who looked into the future as into the past. He was a comrade of Hector's – they were born on the same night – but he was the champion in debate, Hector in battle. He had their interests at heart as he rose and addressed them:

'Consider both sides of the question very carefully, my

friends. It is my opinion that, at this distance from the walls, we ought to withdraw into the town now and not wait for daylight here in the open by the ships. So long as Achilles was at loggerheads with lord Agamemnon, the Greeks were easier to deal with, and I too enjoyed the night we spent beside the ships and the hopes we entertained of capturing their rolling ships. But now I am terrified of swift-footed Achilles. He is a proud man. He will never be content to stay in the plain, where we and the Greeks meet each other on equal terms, but will make our very town and womenfolk his target.

'Believe me, we must now retreat to Ilium. Otherwise, I know what will happen. For the moment, the blessed night has checked Achilles. But if tomorrow he charges out in full armour and catches us here, well, you won't find him hard to recognize. The man who gets away from him and reaches sacred Ilium will thank his stars. It's Trojan flesh the dogs and vultures will be feasting on.

'I pray my words are not an omen! But if, despite your misgivings, you follow my advice, we will keep our army together in the market-place tonight, while the town will be safely protected by its walls, high gateways and great wooden doors fitted to them, firmly closed. At daybreak, fully armed, we will take our position along the battlements; and if Achilles wants to leave the ships and take us on round the walls, so much the worse for him. When he has exhausted his high-necked horses trotting them up and down below the walls, he will have to drive them back to the ships again. However great his anger, it will not allow him to force his way inside. He will never sack the town. The swift dogs will have him first.'

Hector of the flashing helmet gave him a black look and said:

'Polydamas, the man who tells us to retreat and shut ourselves up in the town no longer talks my language. Aren't you sick of being cooped up inside those walls? There was a time when the wealth of Priam's town, its gold and bronze, was the talk of all the world. But that has passed. Our houses have been emptied of their treasure; most of it has been bartered away to Phrygia and lovely Maeonia, since great Zeus came to hate us. Now, at the very moment when the son of sickle-wielding Cronus has allowed me to win glory by the ships and drive the Greeks back against the sea, don't put such notions in the people's heads, you ignorant fool. Not that a single Trojan will follow your lead anyway. I'll see to that.

'So I suggest we all do what I now propose. Let the whole army eat in its several contingents, not forgetting to mount guard and the need for every man to keep alert. As for any Trojan who is over-anxious about his possessions, he should collect them and give them to the people to grow fat on – better for the people to enjoy them than the Greeks! At daybreak, fully armed, we will unleash the dogs of war by their hollow ships. If god-like Achilles really has returned to battle by the ships, so much the worse for him, if that's what he wants. I'm not going to shirk a fight and run away from him. I shall meet him face to face and we shall see who wins the victory. The War-god has no favourites and kills the would-be killer.'

So Hector addressed them, and the Trojans shouted their approval, the fools. Pallas Athene had destroyed their judgement. Polydamas, whose strategy was sound, received no support at all, but they applauded Hector and his bad advice. And now the whole army settled down to eat.

All night long the Greeks lamented and mourned for Patroclus. Achilles son of Peleus was their leader in the loud dirge. He laid his man-slaying hands on his companion's chest and groaned again and again, like a bearded lion when a huntsman has stolen its cubs from a thicket: it comes back too late, grieves for its loss and follows the man's trail through glade after glade, hoping to track him down, and bitter anger overwhelms it – so, groaning heavily, Achilles spoke to his Myrmidons:

'What a fool I was! They were idle words I let fall that day when I was reassuring Patroclus' warrior father Menoetius in Peleus' palace. I said I would bring back his famous son to him at Opous after the sack of Ilium, laden with his share of plunder. But Zeus makes havoc of the schemes of men; and now both of us are destined to redden with our blood one patch of earth here in the land of Troy. I shall never be welcomed again on my return home by Peleus the old charioteer and my mother Thetis, but the earth I stand on will cover me.

'So then, Patroclus, since I too am going below, but after you, I shall not hold your funeral till I have brought back here the armour and the head of Hector, who slaughtered you in your greatness. And at your pyre I am going to cut the throats of a dozen splendid sons of Troy, to vent my anger at your death.

'Till then, you shall lie as you are by my beaked ships, lamented and mourned for day and night by the Trojan women and full-girdled daughters of Dardanus whom we worked hard to capture, with our own hands and our long spears, when we sacked the fertile towns of men.'

With these words godlike Achilles told his companions to stand a great three-legged cauldron over the fire and wash the congealed blood from Patroclus' body as soon as possible. They set a large cauldron over the glowing fire, filled it with water and brought wood for kindling underneath it. The flames began to lick the belly of the cauldron, and the water grew warm. When it came to the boil in the gleaming bronze, they washed the body, anointed it with olive oil and filled the wounds with an ointment nine years old. Then they laid it on a bier and covered it from head to foot with a fine linen cloth, over which they spread a white cloak. And for the rest of the night the Myrmidons gathered round swift-footed Achilles to lament and mourn for Patroclus.

Zeus spoke to his wife and sister Hera:

'So you have had your way once more, ox-eyed lady Hera, and roused swift-footed Achilles. Anyone might think the long-haired Greeks were children of your own.'

Ox-eyed lady Hera replied:

'Dread son of Cronus, what are you suggesting now? Surely even a human, a mere mortal not equipped with such wisdom as ours, is likely to get what he wants on someone else's behalf. How then could I, who claim to be the greatest of goddesses both by right of birth and also because I am your acknowledged wife and you are lord of all the gods – how could I in my rage at the Trojans possibly refrain from making trouble for them?'

While they were talking together in this way, silver-footed Thetis made her way to the starry palace of Hephaestus, which the little club-foot god had built, with his own hands, of imperishable bronze; it shone out among the houses of the gods. She found Hephaestus hard at work and sweating as he bustled about at the bellows in his forge. He was making a set of twenty tripods to stand round the walls of his well-built hall. He had fitted golden wheels to all their feet so that they could run off to a meeting of the gods and return home again, all self-propelled – an amazing sight. They were not quite finished: he still had to put on the ornamental handles and was fitting these and forging the rivets.

Hephaestus was engaged on this task, which called for all his skill, when the goddess silver-footed Thetis arrived. Charis, the famous lame god's wife, beautiful in her shimmering head-dress, came out of the house and saw her. Putting her hand in Thetis', she said:

'Long-robed Thetis, what brings you to our house? You are an honoured and welcome guest, though previously you have not been in the habit of visiting us. But come with me indoors and let me offer you hospitality.'

With these words the celestial goddess led her in and seated her on a beautiful, decorated silver chair with a footstool underneath. Then she called to Hephaestus the famous blacksmith and said:

'Hephaestus! Come here! Thetis wants to ask a favour of you.'

The famous lame god replied:

'Thetis here? The very goddess whom I revere and honour for saving me in my hour of distress when my mother, the bitch, wanted to get rid of me because I was a cripple and threw me out of the skies into the sea! How I would have suffered then, if the sea-goddesses, Thetis and Eurynome daughter of Ocean with its circling stream, hadn't taken me to their hearts! I stayed nine years with them making metal jewellery – brooches, earrings, rosettes and necklaces – there in their vaulted cave, lapped by the never-ending Stream of Ocean seething with foam. No one on earth or in Olympus knew the secret but Eurynome and Thetis who had rescued me. And here is Thetis in our house, lovely-haired Thetis! I must certainly repay her for saving me. Entertain her hospitably, till I have put away my bellows and all my tools.'

Hephaestus spoke and raised his monstrous, panting bulk from the anvil. He limped, but he was nimble enough on his stunted legs. He turned the bellows away from the fire, collected all the tools he used and put them in a silver chest. Then he sponged both sides of his face, his hands, his solid neck and hairy chest, put on his tunic, picked up a thick staff and came limping from the forge.

Waiting-women hurried along to help their master. They were made of gold, but looked like real girls and could not only speak and use their limbs but were also endowed with intelligence and had learned their skills from the immortal gods. While they scurried round to support their lord, Hephaestus moved unsteadily to where Thetis was seated, himself sat down on a polished chair and putting his hand in hers said:

'Long-robed Thetis, what brings you to our house? You are an honoured and a welcome guest, though previously you have not been in the habit of visiting us. Tell me what is in your mind, and I shall gladly do what you ask of me, if I can and if the task is not impossible.'

Bursting into tears, Thetis replied:

'Hephaestus, of all the goddesses on Olympus, is there a single one who has had such anguish and misery to endure as I have, beyond all others, at the hands of Zeus? I, to begin with, was the Sea-nymph whom he picked out from all the rest to force into marrying a human, Peleus son of Aeacus; and much against my will I had to endure the bed of a mortal, who lies at home now, crushed by miserable old age. But Zeus had more to follow. He gave me a son to bear and bring up, greatest of warriors. I nursed him as one tends a little plant in a garden bed and he shot up like a sapling. I sent him to Ilium in his ships to fight against the Trojans; and never again now shall I welcome him home to Peleus' house. And yet he has to suffer, every day he lives and sees the sun; and I can do no good by going to his side.

'Now lord Agamemnon has taken from his arms the girl the Greek army gave him as a prize. He has been eating his heart out in grief at her absence. In consequence the Trojans have been able to pin the Greeks back among their ships, from which they will not let them move. Greek ambassadors were sent to supplicate Achilles and listed many prestigious gifts. But he refused them: he was not going to save them from disaster himself. However, he lent his armour to Patroclus and sent him out into battle with a strong force behind him. They fought all day by the Scaean gate and would have sacked Ilium that very day, if Apollo had not given Hector the glory by killing brave Patroclus in the front line, after he had made havoc of the Trojan ranks.

'So I have come to throw myself at your knees and ask you to give my son, who is so soon to die, a shield and helmet, a pair of fine leg-guards for his shins fitted with ankle-clasps, and body-armour. His former set of armour was lost when his loyal companion was overwhelmed by the Trojans; and Achilles is lying on the ground, pouring his heart out over him.'

The famous lame god replied:

'Take heart. Don't worry about any of this. I only wish it were as easy for me to save him from the pains of death when dread destiny confronts him, as to provide him with a magnificent set of armour, which will be the wonder of everyone who sees it.'

With these words Hephaestus left her there and went back to his forge, where he turned the bellows on the fire and told them to get to work. The bellows – there were twenty of them – blew through the nozzles and gave healthy blasts from different directions, fast or slow to suit the needs of the busy blacksmith, depending on the stage the work had reached. He then placed in the crucibles over the fire imperishable bronze and some tin and precious gold and silver. Then he put a great anvil on its stand and gripped a powerful hammer in one hand and a pair of tongs in the other.

He began by making a large and heavy shield, which he decorated all over and round which he placed a bright triple rim of gleaming metal and fitted with a silver shoulder-strap. The shield consisted of five layers, and he made all sorts of decorations for it, executed with consummate skill.

He made earth, sky and sea, the tireless sun, the full moon and all the constellations with which the skies are crowned, the Pleiades, the Hyades, great Orion and the Bear, also called the waggon. This is the only constellation never to bathe in Ocean Stream, but always wheels round in the same place and looks across at Orion the Hunter with a wary eye.

Next he made two beautiful towns full of people. In one of them weddings and feasts were in progress. They were bringing the brides through the streets from their homes, accompanied by blazing torches, and the wedding-hymn could be heard loud and clear. Young men danced, whirling round to the sound of pipes and lyres, and women stood by the doors of their houses to admire the sight.

But the men had gathered in the meeting-place, where a dispute had arisen between two men who were in conflict about the compensation for a man who had been killed. One side claimed the right to solve the problem by meeting the demand, and was showing the people the full extent of his offer; but the other refused all compensation. Both parties insisted that the issue should be settled by an expert; and both sides were cheered by their supporters in the crowd, whom the heralds were attempting to control. The expert elders sat on smooth stone seats in a sacred circle; they received in their hands the speaker's staff from the clear-voiced heralds; and the two sides rushed over to them as they each gave judgment in turn. Two talents of gold – one from each side – were displayed in the centre: they were the fee for the elder who delivered the soundest judgment.

The other town was under siege from two armies, which were shown in their glittering armour. The besiegers were unable to agree whether to sack the place outright, or to take half the goods that the lovely town contained in return for surrender. But the townspeople had not yet given up: they were secretly preparing an ambush. Leaving the walls defended by their wives and little children, together with the older men, they advanced under the leadership of Ares and Pallas Athene. These were gold, wore golden clothes and looked as big and beautiful in their armour as gods should, standing out above their troops who were on a smaller scale. When the townsmen had found a likely place for an ambush in a river-bed where all the cattle came to drink, they sat down there in their shining bronze armour and posted two scouts in the distance to watch for the arrival of the sheep and cattle with their crooked horns belonging to the besieging army. These soon appeared in the charge of two herdsmen, who were playing on their pipes and suspected no trap.

The men who had laid the ambush saw them, charged out and promptly rounded up the herds of oxen and the fine flocks of white sheep, killing the shepherds. But when the besiegers, who were sitting in debate, heard the commotion raised by this attack on their herds, they immediately mounted the chariots behind their high-stepping horses and made for the scene of action, which they quickly reached. A pitched battle ensued on the banks of the river, and volleys of bronze spears were exchanged. Strife and Panic were co-operating, and there was the dreadful Demon of Death, laying her hands on a freshly wounded man who was still alive and on another not yet wounded, and dragging a body by its foot through the crowd. The cloak on her shoulders was red with human blood; and the warriors met and fought and dragged away each other's dead, just as real warriors do.

Next he placed on it a large field of soft, rich fallow, ploughed three times. A number of ploughmen were driving their teams of oxen across it, up and down. When they reached the ridge at the end of the field and had to turn, a man would come up and hand them a cup of delicious wine. Then they turned back down the furrows, keen to reach the other end through the deep fallow soil. The field, though it was made of gold, grew black behind them, as a field does when it is being ploughed. It was a miraculous piece of work.

He also placed on it a lord's estate where hired reapers were at work with sharp sickles in their hands. Handfuls of corn were falling to the ground one after the other along the lines cut by the reapers, while others were being tied up with bindings by the sheaf-binders following behind. There were three sheaf-binders at work, and boys were at hand, promptly picking up the sheaves and carrying them off in their arms to be stored. And there among them was the lord himself, staff in hand, standing quietly by the point the reapers had reached, delighted. Under an oak-tree some way from the reaping, his attendants were preparing a feast. They were busy with a great ox they had slaughtered, and the women were sprinkling the meat with handfuls of white barley for the labourers' supper.

Next he placed on it a vineyard laden with grapes. It was beautiful and made of gold, but the bunches of grapes were black, and the supporting poles showed up throughout in silver. All round it, Hephaestus ran a ditch of blue inlay and, outside that, a fence of tin. There was a single pathway by which the pickers approached the vineyard to gather the vintage; and young girls and light-hearted boys were carrying off the delicious fruit in baskets. In the middle of them a boy was playing delightfully on a tuneful lyre and singing the song of Linus, quite beautifully, in a high voice. They all kept time with him and followed, singing and shouting, with dancing feet.

He created a herd of straight-horned cattle, making the animals of gold and tin. They were mooing as they hurried from the byre to feed where the rushes swayed beside a murmuring stream. Four golden herdsmen marched with the cattle, and there were nine swift dogs accompanying them. But at the head of the herd a pair of fearsome lions had seized a bellowing bull that roared aloud as it was being dragged off. The young men and dogs were running up to the rescue. But the lions had torn open the great bull's hide and were lapping up its dark blood and entrails. It was in vain that the shepherds were setting their swift dogs on them and urging them forward: when it came to sinking their teeth into the lions, the dogs were having none of it. They stood there at close range, barking, but were careful to avoid them.

The famous lame god created a big grazing ground for white-fleeced sheep, in a beautiful valley, with farm buildings, pens and well-roofed huts.

Next the famous lame god cleverly depicted a dancing-floor, like the one Daedalus designed in the spacious town of Cnossus for lovely-haired Ariadne. Youths and marriageable maidens were dancing there holding each other by the wrists, the girls in fine linen shawls, the men in closely woven tunics showing a faint gleam of oil, the girls with lovely garlands on their heads, the men with daggers of gold hanging from their silver belts. Here they circled lightly round on accomplished feet, like the wheel which fits neatly in a potter's hands when he sits down and tests it to see if it will spin; and here they ran in lines to meet each other. A large crowd stood round enjoying the delightful dance. A godlike singer of tales sang with them to the lyre, while a couple of solo dancers led off and spun round among the people.

Then, round the very rim of the superbly constructed shield, he placed the mighty Stream of Ocean.

When he had finished the great, heavy shield, he

made Achilles' body-armour brighter than blazing fire. Then he made a massive helmet to fit on his temples. It was beautifully decorated, and he put a gold crest on top. He also made him leg-guards of soft tin for his shins.

When the famous lame god had finished every piece, he gathered them up and laid them before Achilles' mother. She took the glittering armour from Hephaestus in her arms and swooped down like a falcon from snow-clad Olympus.

The Death of Hector (Book 22)

Achilles returns to the slaughter and drives the Trojans back into Troy, leaving Hector alone to face him outside the walls.

So the Trojans, running for it like fawns, took refuge in the town. There they dried the sweat off their bodies, drank and slaked their thirst as they leant against the fine battlements, while the Greeks advanced on the wall, their shields at the slope on their shoulders. But deadly destiny shackled Hector where he was, outside Ilium in front of the Scaean gate.

Meanwhile Phoebus Apollo spoke to Achilles:

'Son of Peleus, why are you chasing me on those swift feet of yours? You are a man, and I an immortal god, as you might have noticed, had you not been so preoccupied with your pursuit. But surely you must be neglecting your business with the Trojans you put to flight. Look, they've shut themselves up in the town, while you have been side-tracked all the way out here. But you'll never kill *me*: I, naturally, am not marked out for death.'

Furious, swift-footed Achilles replied:

'You've made a fool of me, Apollo, most malevolent of all the gods, by luring me out here away from the walls. To think of all the Trojans who would otherwise have bitten the dust and not reached Ilium! You have robbed me of a great victory by saving their lives, an easy task for you, who have no retribution to fear. I would certainly pay you back, if only I had the power.'

With these words Achilles made fearlessly for the town, racing along like a prize-winning horse galloping effortlessly at speed over the plain with its chariot. So lightly and easily Achilles sprinted off.

Old Priam was the first to see him, shining like a star as he sped across the plain – like the star that comes in autumn, outshining all its fellows in the evening sky. They call it Orion's Dog, and though it is the brightest of all stars, it heralds no good, bringing much fever, as it does, to wretched mortals. That was how the bronze gleamed on Achilles' chest as he ran.

The old man gave a groan. He lifted up his hands and beat his head. With a great cry he shouted in supplication to his beloved son Hector, who had taken his stand in front of the gates, implacable in his determination to fight it out with Achilles. Stretching out his arms, the old man piteously addressed him:

'Hector, I beg you, my dear son, don't stand up to that man alone and without help. You are inviting defeat and death at his hands. He is far stronger than you and quite ruthless. The dogs and vultures would soon be feeding on his body (and what a load that would lift from my heart!) if only the gods loved him as little as I do – the man who has robbed me of so many splendid sons, killed them or sold them off as slaves to distant islands.

'There are still two of them I cannot find among the troops huddling in the town, Lycaon and Polydorus, children of mine by my mistress, lady Laothoe. If the enemy have taken them alive, we will ransom them presently with bronze and gold, of which there is plenty inside, since old Altes, Laothoe's famous father, gave his daughter a massive dowry. But if they are dead by now and in the halls of Hades, there will be one more sorrow for me and their mother who brought them into the world, even though the rest of Ilium will not mourn for them so long – unless you join them and also fall to Achilles. So come inside the walls, my son, to be the saviour of Trojan men and women; and do not throw away your own precious life to give a triumph to the son of Peleus.

'Have pity too on me, your poor father, while I still live my ill-fated existence, since Father Zeus has kept in store for my old age a hideous fate, innumerable horrors I shall have to see before I die – sons massacred, daughters raped, bedrooms pillaged, little babies hurled ruthlessly to the ground and killed, my sons' wives hauled away by murderous Greek hands.

'Last of all my turn will come after someone's spear or sword has removed the life from these limbs; and my dogs, turned savage, tear me to pieces at the entrance to my palace. The very dogs I have fed at table and trained to watch my gate will lie in front of my doors, restlessly lapping their master's blood. It looks well enough for a young man killed in battle to lie there mutilated by a sharp spear: death can find nothing to expose in him that is not beautiful. But when an old man's dogs defile his grey head, his grey beard and his genitals, wretched mortals plumb the depths of human misery.'

The old man spoke and tore at his grey locks and pulled the hair from his head; but he did not shake Hector's resolve. And now his mother Hecabe in her turn began to lament and weep. Drawing open the folds of her dress, she held up her breast in her hand and, with the tears running down her cheeks, spoke winged words:

'Hector, my son, have some respect for this and pity me, if ever I gave you this breast to soothe away your troubles! Remember those days, dear child. Deal with your enemy from here inside the walls and do not go out to meet that man in single combat. He is ruthless; and if he kills you, I shall never lay you out on a bier and weep for you, dear child of my flesh, nor will your wife, however rich her dowry; but far away from both of us beside the Greek ships the swift dogs will consume you.'

So they spoke in tears to their dear son. But all their entreaties did not shake Hector's resolve: he stayed where he was, awaiting the approach of awe-inspiring Achilles. As a mountain snake waits for a man beside its hole: it has swallowed poisonous herbs, its anger is dreadful and it stares intimidatingly at him, wreathing its coils round its lair – so Hector, his determination unquenchable, refused to retreat. He leaned his glittering shield against the projecting tower and, deeply troubled, reflected on the situation:

'What am I to do? If I retire behind the gate and the wall, Polydamas will be the first to point the finger of blame at me that, on this last accursed night when godlike Achilles rose up again, I did not take his advice and order a withdrawal into the town. It would have been much better if I had. As it is, having sacrificed the army to my own reckless stupidity, I would feel nothing but shame before the Trojan men and the Trojan women in their trailing gowns. I could not bear to hear some second-rater say: "Hector trusted in his own right arm and lost an army." But it *will* be said, and then it would be far better for me to stand up to Achilles and either kill him and come home alive, or be killed by him gloriously in front of Ilium.

'If I put down my bossed shield and heavy helmet, prop my spear against the wall and approach matchless Achilles myself . . . if I promise to return Helen and all her property with her . . . everything in fact that Paris brought away with him to Troy in his hollow ships, which was how this war started . . . to give it all to Agamemnon and Menelaus to take away, and to divide up everything else with the Greeks as well, everything the town possesses . . . and then if I take an oath with the elders in council on behalf of the Trojans not to hide anything but to divide it all up equally, all the property our lovely town contains . . .

'But why talk to myself like this? If I approach Achilles as a suppliant, he'll show me no pity, no respect. He'll kill me out of hand, exposed as I will be when I take off my armour, like a woman. I can't somehow see Achilles and myself engaging in intimacies "from an oak or a rock", as a girl and boy do, a girl and boy, just the two, with their intimacies. No: better to waste no time and come to grips. Let's find out to which of us the Olympian intends to hand the victory.'

As Hector paused and considered the matter, Achilles

came on at him, looking like the god of war, the warrior with the nodding helmet. Over his right shoulder he was brandishing the formidable ash spear from Mount Pelion, and his bronze armour glowed like a blazing fire or the rising sun. Hector saw him and shook. He could not stand his ground; he left the gate and ran in panic. But the son of Peleus, counting on his speed, was after him. Like a mountain hawk, the fastest thing on wings, when it effortlessly swoops after a timid dove; under and away the dove dives off, and the hawk, shrieking close behind, strikes at it again and again in its determination to make a kill – so Achilles started off in hot pursuit, and Hector fled in terror before him under the walls of Ilium, fast as his feet would go.

Passing the lookout-post and the windswept fig-tree and always keeping some way from the wall, they sped along the waggon-track and came to the two sweet-flowing springs that are the sources of Scamander's eddying stream. In one of these the water comes up hot; steam rises from it like smoke from a blazing fire. But the other, even in summer, gushes up like hail or freezing snow or water that has turned to ice. Close beside them, wide and beautiful, stand the stone washing-places where the wives and lovely daughters of the Trojans used to wash their shining clothes in earlier days, when there was peace, before the coming of the Greeks.

Here the two raced past, Hector in flight and Achilles after him – a fine man in front but a far stronger one at his heels. And the pace was furious. They were not running for the usual prize at a foot-race, a sacrificial beast or leather shield: they were competing for the life of horse-taming Hector. As powerful prize-winning race-horses corner at speed round a turning-post: a great prize has been set up, a tripod or a woman, in honour of a warrior who has died – so the pair of them circled three times round Priam's town, feet flying.

All the gods were looking on. The Father of men and gods then began and spoke his mind:

'This is an unhappy business! I have a warm place in my heart for this man who is being chased before my eyes round the walls of Ilium. I grieve for Hector. He has burnt the thighs of many oxen in my honour, on the heights of Mount Ida with its many ridges and on the lofty citadel of Ilium. But now godlike Achilles is pursuing him at full speed round Priam's town. Consider, gods, and help me to decide whether we shall save his life, or let a good man fall this day to Achilles son of Peleus.'

The goddess grey-eyed Athene replied:

'Father, lord of the vivid lightning, god of the dark cloud, what are you talking about? Are you proposing to reprieve from the pains of death a mortal man whose destiny has long been settled? Do what you like, then; but not all the rest of us gods will approve.'

Zeus who marshals the clouds replied and said:

'Have no fear, Triton-born Athene, dear child. I was not in earnest and do not mean to be unkind to you. Act as you see fit, and act at once.'

So he spoke, and encouraged Athene, who had already set her heart on action, and she came swooping down from the heights of Olympus.

Meanwhile swift Achilles continued his relentless pursuit of Hector. As a hound starts a fawn from its mountain covert and pursues it through the glens and valleys: even when it takes cover in a thicket, the dog continues to track it until it finds it – so Hector could not shake off swift-footed Achilles. More than once, Hector made a move towards the Dardanian gate, hoping to get close enough under the well-built towers for those above to protect him with their missiles; but Achilles, hugging the inside path, intercepted him every time and headed him off towards the plain.

Like a chase in a nightmare when no one, pursuer or pursued, can move a limb, so Achilles could not catch up Hector, nor Hector shake off Achilles. How could Hector have escaped the demons of death, had not Apollo come to him for the last time and given him new drive and fresh speed? Achilles too had been signalling to his men with his head not to shoot at Hector, in case someone else hit him and won the glory, and he came second.

But when they reached the springs for the fourth time, the Father held out his golden scales and, putting death that lays men low in either pan, on one side for Achilles, on the other for horse-taming Hector, raised the balance by the middle of the beam. The beam came down on Hector's side, spelling his doom. He was on his way to Hades. Phoebus Apollo deserted him; and the goddess grey-eyed Athene came up to Achilles and, standing beside him, spoke winged words:

'Now, glorious Achilles dear to Zeus, our chance has come to go back to the ships with a great victory for the

Greeks. Hector is hungry for battle, but you and I are going to kill him. There is no escape for him from us now, however much humiliation the Archer-god Apollo endures, grovelling abjectly at the feet of his Father Zeus who drives the storm-cloud. You stay here now and recover your breath, while I go to Hector and persuade him to fight you.'

So spoke Athene, and Achilles was delighted and did as she told him. He stood there, leaning on his bronze-barbed spear, while Athene went across from him to godlike Hector, borrowing the appearance and tireless voice of his brother Deiphobus. She came up to Hector and spoke winged words:

'My dear brother, swift Achilles has certainly been pressing you hard, chasing you at that speed round the town. Let's make a stand and keep him off together.'

Great Hector of the flashing helmet replied to her:

'Deiphobus, you were always by far the closest of all the brothers Hecabe and Priam gave me. But now I shall think even better of you, since you had the courage, when you saw the situation, to come outside the walls and help me, while all the rest stayed inside.'

The goddess grey-eyed Athene replied:

'Dear brother, our father and lady mother took my knees and, one after the other, entreated me to stay where I was. My men were there and did the same – they are all in such terror of Achilles. But I was tormented by anxiety on your behalf. Now let's make a determined attack, straight at him, and no restraint with the spears! We'll soon find out whether Achilles is to kill the pair of us and go off with our bloodstained armour to the hollow ships, or himself be conquered by your spear.'

With these words Athene treacherously led him forward. When Hector and Achilles came within range of each other, great Hector of the flashing helmet spoke first:

'Achilles, I'm not going to run from you any more. I have already been chased by you three times round Priam's great town without daring to stop and let you come near. But now I have made up my mind to fight you man to man and kill you or be killed.

'But let us call on the gods to witness an agreement: no compact could have better guarantors. If Zeus grants me staying-power and I kill you, I will not violently maltreat you. All I shall do, Achilles, is to strip you of your famous armour. Then I will give up your body to the Greeks. You do the same.'

Swift-footed Achilles gave him a black look and replied:

'Hector, I'm never going to forgive you. So don't talk to me about agreements. Lions don't come to terms with men, the wolf doesn't see eye to eye with the lamb – they are enemies to the end. It's the same with you and me. Friendship between us is impossible, and there will be no truce of any kind till one of us has fallen and glutted the shield-bearing god of battles with his blood.

'So summon up all the courage you possess. This is the time to show your bravery and ability as a fighter. Not that anything is going to save you now, when Pallas Athene is waiting to bring you down with my spear. This moment you are going to pay the full price for all the sufferings of my companions you killed on your rampage with your spear.'

He spoke, balanced his long-shadowed spear and hurled it. But glorious Hector was on the lookout and avoided the bronze spear. He crouched, his eye on the weapon, and it flew over him and stuck in the ground. But Pallas Athene snatched it up and brought it back to Achilles without Hector shepherd of the people noticing. Hector spoke to the matchless son of Peleus:

'You missed! So, godlike Achilles, Zeus gave you the wrong date for my death after all! You thought you knew everything. But then you're so glib, so clever with your tongue – trying to frighten me and undermine my determination and courage. But you won't make me run and then hit me in the back with your spear. Drive it through my chest as I charge – if the god lets you. But first you will have to avoid this one of mine. May the whole length of it find a home in your body! This war would be an easier business for the Trojans if you, their greatest scourge, were dead.'

He spoke, balanced his long-shadowed spear and hurled it. He hit the centre of Achilles' shield and did not miss, but the spear rebounded from it. Hector was frustrated that the swift spear had left his hand to no purpose and stood there dismayed, since he had no other one. He shouted aloud to Deiphobus of the white shield, asking him for a long spear. But Deiphobus was nowhere near him. Hector realized what had happened and said:

'It's over. So the gods did, after all, summon me to my death. I thought the warrior Deiphobus was at my side. But he is behind the wall, and Athene has deceived me. Evil death is no longer far away; it is staring me in the face and there is no escape. Zeus and his Archer son must long have been resolved on this, for all their earlier goodwill and help.

'So now my destiny confronts me. Let me at least sell my life dearly and not without glory, after some great deed for future generations to hear of.'

With these words Hector drew the sharp, long, heavy sword hanging down at his side. He gathered himself and swooped like a high-flying eagle that drops to earth through black clouds to pounce on a tender lamb or cowering hare. So Hector swooped, brandishing his sharp sword.

Achilles sprang to meet him, his heart filled with savage determination. He kept his chest covered with his fine, ornate shield; his glittering helmet with its four plates nodded, and above it danced the lovely plumes that Hephaestus had lavished on the crest. Like a star moving with others through the night, Hesperus, the loveliest star set in the skies – such was the gleam from his spear's sharp point as he weighed it in his right hand with murder in his heart for godlike Hector, searching that handsome body for its most vulnerable spot.

Hector's body was completely covered by the fine bronze armour he had taken from great Patroclus when he killed him, except for the flesh that could be seen at the windpipe, where the collar bones hold the neck from the shoulders, the easiest place to kill a man. As Hector charged him, godlike Achilles drove at this spot with his spear, and the point went right through Hector's soft neck, though the heavy bronze head did not cut his windpipe and left him still able to speak. Hector crashed in the dust, and godlike Achilles triumphed over him:

'Hector, no doubt you imagined, as you stripped Patroclus, that you would be safe. You never thought of me: I was too far away. You innocent. Down by the hollow ships a man much better than Patroclus had been left behind. It was I, and I have brought you down. So now the dogs and birds of prey are going to mangle you foully, while we Greeks will give Patroclus full burial honours.'

Fading fast, Hector of the flashing helmet replied:

'I entreat you, by your knees, by your own life, and by your parents, do not throw my body to the dogs by the Greek ships but take a ransom for me. My father and my lady mother will give you bronze and gold in plenty. Give up my body to be brought home, so that the Trojans and their wives can cremate it properly.'

Swift-footed Achilles gave him a black look and replied:

'You dog, don't entreat me by my knees or my parents. I only wish I could summon up the will to carve and eat you raw myself, for what you have done to me. But this at least is certain: nobody is going to keep the dogs off your head, not even if the Trojans bring here and weigh out a ransom ten or twenty times your worth, and promise more besides; not even if Dardanian Priam tells them to offer your weight in gold – not even so shall your lady mother lay you on a bier to mourn the son she bore, but the dogs and birds of prey will divide you up, leaving nothing.'

Dying, Hector of the flashing helmet said:

'How well I know you and see you for what you are! Your heart is hard as iron. I have been wasting my breath. But reflect now before you act, in case angry gods remember how you treated me, on the day Paris and Phoebus Apollo bring you down in all your greatness at the Scaean gate.'

As he spoke, the end that is death enveloped him. Life left his limbs and took wing for the house of Hades, bewailing its lot and the youth and the manhood it had left behind. But godlike Achilles spoke to him again, though he was gone:

'Die! As for my death, I will welcome it when Zeus and the other immortal gods wish it to be.'

He spoke, withdrew his bronze spear from the body and put it on one side. As he removed the bloodstained arms from Hector's shoulders, other Greeks came running up and gathered round. They gazed in wonder at the stature and marvellous good looks of Hector. As each went in and stabbed the body, they looked at each other and said as one man:

'Well, well! Hector's certainly softer to handle now than when he set the ships on fire!'

So they spoke, as they stood by, stabbing him. After stripping Hector, swift-footed godlike Achilles stood up among the Greeks and spoke winged words:

'My friends, rulers and leaders of the Greeks, now that the gods have let us get the better of this man, who did more damage than all the rest together, let's make a circuit of the town under arms and find out what the

Trojans mean to do next, whether they will abandon their town now that Hector is fallen, or make up their minds to hold it without his help . . .

'But why talk to myself like this? Lying by my ships is a dead man, unburied, unwept – Patroclus, whom I shall never forget as long as I am among the living and can walk the earth, my own dear comrade, whom I shall still remember even though the dead forget their dead, even in Hades' halls. So come now, young Greeks, let us go back to the hollow ships carrying this body and singing a song of triumph. We have won great glory. We have killed godlike Hector, who was treated like a god in Ilium.'

He spoke and foully maltreated godlike Hector. He sliced into the tendons at the back of both his feet between the heel and ankle, inserted leather straps and tied them to his chariot, leaving the head to drag. Then he lifted his famous armour into the chariot, got in himself, and lashed the horses with the whip to get them moving. The willing pair flew off. Dust rose from the body they dragged behind them; Hector's sable hair streamed out on either side and his whole head, so graceful once, lay in the dirt. Zeus now let his enemies disfigure him in the very own land of his fathers.

So his whole head was enveloped in the dust. When his mother saw her son, she tore her hair, hurled her bright head-dress far away and screamed aloud. His father groaned piteously, the people round them took up the cry of grief and the whole town gave itself up to despair. It was as if the whole of frowning Ilium were smouldering from top to bottom. The stricken old man made for the Dardanian gate, determined on going out, and when the people only just managed to stop him, he grovelled in the dung and implored them all, calling on each man by name:

'Friends, hold off. I know your concern for me, but let me go out of the town alone to the Greek ships. I want to supplicate this inhuman monster, who may perhaps feel respect for my years and pity my old age. After all, he too has a father of the same age as myself, Peleus, who gave him life and brought him up to be the scourge of all Trojans, though none of them has suffered at his hands so much as I, the father of so many sons butchered by him in their prime.

'And yet, though I weep for them all, there is one I mourn still more with a bitter sorrow that will bring me to the grave – Hector. If only he could have died in my arms! Then we could have wept and lamented for him to our hearts' content, I and the mother who brought him, to her sorrow, into the world.'

So he spoke in tears, and the people took up the cry. Now Hecabe led the Trojan women in a shrill lament:

'My child! Ah, misery me! Why should I live and suffer now you are dead? Night and day in Ilium you were the answer to my prayers, and to every man and woman in the town a dream come true, a man they greeted like a god. You were their greatest glory while you lived. Now death and destiny have claimed you.'

So Hecabe spoke in tears. But Hector's wife Andromache had not yet heard the news. No reliable messenger had in fact gone to tell her that her husband had remained outside the gates. She was at work in a corner of her lofty house on a web of purple cloth to be folded double, and weaving flowers into it. She had just called to the lovely-haired waiting-women in her house to put a large cauldron on the fire so that Hector could have a hot bath when he came home from the battle – the innocent. She never dreamed that, far away from any baths, grey-eyed Athene had killed him at Achilles' hands.

But now the grief and lamentation at the battlements reached her ears. A tremor went through her and she dropped the shuttle on the floor. She called again to her waiting-women:

'Come with me, two of you: I must see what has happened. That was my husband's mother I heard, and she is a reticent woman. My heart is in my mouth: I am paralysed with fear. Some disaster is threatening the house of Priam. May I never hear such news, but I am terrified that godlike Achilles has caught my daring Hector by himself outside the town and chased him out over the plain; indeed, that he has already put an end to that fatal overconfidence of his. Because Hector would never hang back with the crowd – he always advanced far ahead of the rest, second to none in his courage.'

With these words Andromache, with palpitating heart, rushed out of the house like a mad woman, and her waiting-women went with her. When she came to the tower where the men had gathered in a crowd, she stood on the wall, searched the plain and saw her husband being dragged off in front of the town and the swift horses hauling him unceremoniously away towards the Greek ships.

Black night came down and engulfed Andromache's eyes. She crashed backwards, fainting. The bright head-dress flew far from her head, with the headband, the cap, the woven braids and headscarf that golden Aphrodite had given her on the day when Hector of the flashing helmet, after giving an untold bride-price, came to fetch her from her father Eëtion's house. Her husband's sisters and his brothers' wives crowded round and supported her between them; she was distraught to the point of death. When at length she recovered and came to herself, she burst out sobbing and said to the Trojan women:

'Hector, what unhappiness is mine! So you and I were born under the same star, you here in Priam's house and I in Thebe under the woods of Mount Placus in the house of Eëtion, who brought me up from childhood, the ill-fated father of a more ill-fated child. He should never have fathered me! For you are on your way to Hades under the depths of the earth, leaving me behind in hateful misery, a widow in your house. And your son is no more than a baby, the son we got between us, we unhappy parents. You will be no joy to him, Hector, now you are dead, nor he to you.

'Even if he survives this war with all its tears, nothing remains for him but hardship and distress. Others will take over his lands. An orphaned child is cut off from his friends. He goes about with downcast eyes and tear-stained cheeks. Need drives him to his father's acquaintances, and he tugs a cloak here and a tunic there till someone out of pity holds up a wine-cup briefly to his mouth, just enough to wet his lips but not to drink. Then comes another boy, with both his parents living, who drives him from the feast, punching him and jeering at him: "Go on, get out! You've got no father dining here!" So the child runs off in tears to his widowed mother – the little Astyanax, who used to sit on his father's knees and eat nothing but marrow and mutton fat and, when he was drowsy and tired of play, slept in his bed, softly cradled in his nurse's arms, heart full of contentment. But now with his father gone, suffering will be the lot of Astyanax, "Town-lord", as the Trojans called him, seeing in you, Hector, the one defence of their long walls and gates.

'And you, by the beaked ships, far from your parents, naked, will be eaten by the wriggling worms when the dogs have had their fill. Yet delicate and lovely clothing made by women's hands is still stored at home. I am going to burn it all in the consuming fire. It is of no use to you: you will never even be buried in it. But the men and women of Troy will do that for you as their last mark of honour.'

So she spoke in tears, and the women took up the cry.

Priam and Achilles (Book 24)

Patroclus is buried and funeral games held.

The gathering broke up, and the warriors scattered to their several ships; they were thinking of the pleasures of food and sweet sleep. But Achilles began to weep for his dear companion whom he could not banish from his mind, and all-conquering sleep refused to visit him. He tossed and turned from side to side, always thinking of his loss, of Patroclus' manliness and spirit, of all they had been through together and the hardships they had endured, of battles against the enemy and dangers at sea. As memories crowded in, the warm tears poured down his cheeks. Sometimes he lay on his side, sometimes on his back and then again on his face. Then he would get up and roam agitatedly along the salt-sea beach.

Dawn after dawn as it lit up the sea and coastline never failed to find him there. He would yoke his swift horses to his chariot, tie Hector's body loosely to the back of it and, when he had hauled it three times round Patroclus' grave-mound, go back and rest in his hut, leaving the body stretched face downward in the dust. But dead though Hector was, Apollo still felt pity for the man and protected his flesh from all disfigurement. Moreover, he wrapped him in his golden aegis, so that Achilles should not tear his flesh when he was dragging him along.

So Achilles in his fury disfigured godlike Hector. The blessed gods looked on and took pity on him. They even urged Hermes, sharp-eyed slayer of Argus, to steal the body, but while this found favour with the rest, it had no appeal for Hera, Poseidon or grey-eyed Athene. These hated sacred Ilium and Priam and his people just as much now as when Paris first committed that act of blind folly at the judgement in his shepherd's hut, when he humiliated Hera and Athene by preferring Aphrodite – whose reward was his fatal lust for women.

Eleven days went by, and at dawn on the twelfth Phoebus Apollo spoke out to the immortals:

'You are hard-hearted, you gods – monsters of cruelty. Did Hector never burn for you the thighs of oxen and of unblemished goats? Yet now you will not even go so far as to save his body for his wife, mother and child to see, and for his father Priam and his people to cremate and honour with funeral rites. No, it's the murderous Achilles you gods choose to support, Achilles, who has no decent feelings in him and remains utterly relentless, like a lion that, when it wants its food, looks to nothing but its own great strength and arrogant appetites and pounces on shepherds' flocks. Achilles, like the lion, has destroyed pity; he has no respect for others.

'Many a man, I presume, is likely to have lost an even dearer one than he has, a brother borne by the same mother, or maybe a son. He weeps and laments for him, and that is the end of it, since the fates have endowed men with an enduring heart. But Achilles first robs god-like Hector of his life and then ties him to his chariot and drags him round the tomb of his beloved companion. As though that will do him honour or credit! He had better beware of our anger, great man though he is. All he is doing in his fury is disfiguring dumb clay.'

Angrily, white-armed Hera replied:

'There would be something in what you say, lord of the silver bow, if you gods had it in mind to honour Hector as you do Achilles. But Hector is a mere mortal, who was suckled at a woman's breast; while Achilles is the son of Thetis, a goddess, whom I myself brought up and took under my wing and gave in marriage to a man, to Peleus, the greatest favourite we had. All you gods came to the wedding. And so did *you*, Apollo, and sat down at the wedding feast, lyre in hand. But then you always were two-faced, you and your crooked friends.'

Zeus who marshals the clouds replied and said:

'Hera, stop losing your temper with the gods. There is no question of putting the two men on the same footing. But the fact remains that Hector was our favourite out of everyone in Ilium. He certainly was mine: he never failed to give me what I like. My altar never lacked its share of generous offerings, libations of wine and the fat from burnt sacrifice, the honour gods have been granted as our right. But we must abandon this idea of secretly stealing Hector's body. In any case it is not feasible, since Achilles' mother stays beside him night and day. However, let one of the gods tell Thetis to come here to me. I have a carefully considered solution to suggest, to make Achilles accept a ransom from Priam and release Hector.'

So he spoke, and Iris, quick as the wind, sped off on her mission. Halfway between Samothrace and rugged Imbros she dived into the dark sea, and the waters boomed and echoed. She sank to the bottom like the piece of lead that an angler attaches to his ox-horn lure to bring death to the greedy fish. She found Thetis in her vaulted cavern, surrounded by a gathering of other salt-sea Nymphs; she was in the middle, bewailing the lot of her matchless son, destined, as she knew, to be killed in fertile Troy far from the land of his fathers. Swift-footed Iris came up to her and spoke:

'Come, Thetis. Zeus in his infinite wisdom calls you to his side.'

The goddess silver-footed Thetis replied:

'What does the great god want me for? I am so over-whelmed with sorrow that I shrink from mixing with the gods. However, I will come – Zeus' words will not be idle.'

With these words the goddess took a dark-blue shawl – there was nothing blacker she could wear – and set out on her journey, preceded by swift Iris, quick as the wind. The waters of the sea made way for them, and they came out on the shore and sped up to the skies where they found far-thundering Zeus with all the other blessed everlasting gods seated round him. Thetis sat down by Father Zeus – Athene let her have her chair – and Hera, with a warm word of welcome, passed her a lovely golden cup which Thetis returned to her when she had drunk from it. The Father of men and gods began and spoke his mind:

'So, goddess Thetis, you have come to Olympus in spite of your troubles. You are distraught with grief – I know that as well as you. Nevertheless I must tell you why I called you here. For nine days the gods have been quarrelling over Hector's body and Achilles sacker of cities. They have even urged Hermes, the sharp-eyed slayer of Argus, to steal the body. But I intend to grant Achilles glory and in that way preserve your future respect and goodwill.

'Go at once to the camp and convey my orders to your son. Tell him the gods are displeased with him and that I am the angriest of them all, because in his senseless fury he refuses to part with Hector's body and has kept it by his beaked ships. If he will somehow fear me and release Hector, I will send Iris to great-hearted Priam to suggest that he should ransom his son by going to the Greek ships with gifts for Achilles that will warm his heart.'

So he spoke, and the goddess silver-footed Thetis complied. She came swooping down from the heights of Olympus and reached her son's hut. There she found him, groaning incessantly, while his comrades bustled around him in busy preparation of a meal, for which a large fleecy sheep was being slaughtered. Achilles' lady mother sat down close beside him, stroked him with her hand and spoke to him:

'My child, how much longer are you going to eat your heart out in lamentation and misery, forgetful even of food and bed? It must be a good thing to make love to a woman – you have so short a time to live and already stand in the shadow of death and inexorable destiny.

'Listen to me now and understand I come from Zeus, who wishes you to know the gods are displeased with you and that he himself is the angriest of them all, because in your senseless fury you refuse to part with Hector's body and have kept it by your beaked ships. Come now, give it back and accept a ransom for the dead.'

Swift-footed Achilles replied and said:

'If the Olympian is in earnest and himself commands me, then bring in the man who would offer a ransom and take the body away.'

While mother and son exchanged many a winged word with each other down there among the ships, Zeus dispatched Iris to sacred Ilium:

'Off with you, swift Iris. Leave your Olympian home and take a message to great-hearted Priam in Ilium. Tell him to ransom his son by going to the Greek ships with gifts for Achilles that will warm his heart. He must go alone, without a single Trojan to escort him, except maybe one of the older heralds who could drive the mules and smooth-running waggon and bring back to Ilium the body of the man godlike Achilles killed. Tell him not to think of death and to have no fears whatever. We will send him the best of escorts, Hermes slayer of Argus, who will remain in charge till he has brought him into Achilles' presence. Once he is inside his hut, no one is going to kill him, neither Achilles himself nor anybody else. Achilles will see to that. He is not foolish, thoughtless or wicked. On the contrary, he will spare his suppliant and show him every kindness.'

So he spoke, and Iris, quick as the wind, sped off on

her mission. She came to Priam's palace where sounds of lamentation met her. In the courtyard Priam's sons were sitting round their father, drenching their clothes with tears, and there in the middle sat the old man wrapped up in his cloak, showing just the outline of his body, with his head and neck plastered with the dung he had gathered in his hands as he grovelled on the ground. His daughters and his sons' wives were wailing through the house, remembering the many fine men who had lost their lives at Greek hands and now lay dead.

The messenger of Zeus stood by Priam and addressed him. She spoke in a low voice, but his limbs began at once to tremble:

'Courage, Dardanian Priam! Compose yourself and have no fears. I come here not as a messenger of evil, but of hope. And I am the messenger of Zeus who, far off as he is, is much concerned on your behalf and pities you. The Olympian orders you to ransom godlike Hector with gifts for Achilles that will warm his heart. You must go alone without a single Trojan to escort you, except maybe one of the older heralds who could drive the mules and smooth-running waggon and bring back to Ilium the body of the man godlike Achilles killed. Do not think of death and have no fears whatever. The best of escorts, Hermes slayer of Argus, will remain in charge till he has brought you into Achilles' presence. Once you are inside his hut, no one is going to kill you, neither Achilles himself nor anybody else. Achilles will see to that. He is not foolish, thoughtless or wicked. On the contrary, he will spare his suppliant and show you every kindness.'

With these words swift-footed Iris disappeared. Priam told his sons to get ready a smooth-running mule-waggon with a wicker basket lashed on top. Then he went down to his high-roofed, scented store-room which was built of cedar-wood and was full of treasures. He called out to Hecabe his wife and said:

'My dear, an Olympian messenger has come to me from Zeus and told me to ransom Hector's body by going to the Greek ships with gifts for Achilles that will warm his heart. Tell me, what do you make of that? My own feelings impel me to go down to the ships and pay this visit to the broad Greek camp.'

So he spoke, and his wife shrieked aloud and replied:

'Are you mad? Where is the wisdom which people from abroad and your own subjects used to praise in you? How can you think of going by yourself to the Greek ships into the presence of a man who has killed so many of your fine sons? You must have a heart of iron. Once you are in his power, once he sets his eyes on you – that flesh-eating, faithless savage – he will show you no mercy at all nor the slightest respect.

'No: all we can do now is sit at home and weep for our son from here. This must be the end that inexorable destiny spun for him with the first thread of life when I brought him into the world – to glut the swift dogs, far from his parents, in the clutches of a monster whose very liver I would sink my teeth into and devour. That would pay him back for what he has done to my son, who was not playing the coward when Achilles killed him, but fighting, without any thought of flight or cover, in defence of the sons and full-girdled daughters of Troy.'

Venerable godlike Priam replied:

'I am determined to go. Do not keep me back or turn into a bird of ill-omen in our palace – you will not dissuade me. If any human being, a prophet or a priest, had made me this suggestion, I would have said it was a lie and disregarded it. But I personally heard the goddess' voice: I saw her there in front of me. So I am going and the goddess' words will not be idle. If I am destined to die by the ships of the bronze-armoured Greeks, then I choose death. Achilles can kill me then and there, once I have taken my son in my arms and wept my fill.'

He spoke and lifted the lovely lids of the storage-chests. From these he took out twelve beautiful robes, twelve single cloaks, as many sheets, as many white mantles and as many tunics to go with them. He also weighed and took ten talents of gold; and he took two shining tripods, four cauldrons and a very lovely cup which the Thracians had given him when he went there on a mission. It was a fabulous present, but so great was his desire to ransom his beloved son that the old man did not hesitate to part with it also.

There were a number of Trojans hanging around the portico. Priam drove them all off with a stream of abuse:

'Get out of here, you despicable, worthless wretches! Haven't you enough to weep about in your own homes without intruding on my grief as well? Or wasn't it enough for you that Zeus son of Cronus has afflicted me with the loss of the best of sons? If so, you will soon learn better. The Greeks will find you still easier to deal with now Hector is dead. As for me, I only hope I go down to Hades' halls before I see the town plundered and laid waste.'

He spoke and drove them off with his staff, and they fled from the quick-tempered old man. Next he shouted angrily at his sons, abusing Helenus, Paris and godlike Agathon; Pammon and Antiphonus and Polites master of the battle-cry; Deiphobus, Hippothous and noble Dius. He shouted at all nine of them and told them what to do:

'Move, you miserable, cowardly children of mine! I wish you had all been killed beside the swift ships instead of Hector. Ah, how calamity has dogged my life! I had the best sons in the broad realm of Troy. Now all of them are gone – godlike Mestor, Troilus the charioteer and Hector, a god among mortals, who looked more like a god's son than a man's. The War-god has taken them and left me this disgraceful crew – swindlers and show-offs every one of you, stars of the song-and-dance routine, when you aren't looting your own people of their sheep and kids. Now won't you be so *kind* as to get my waggon ready at once and put in everything I need to see me on my way?'

So he spoke, and his sons were terrified by their father's fulminations and quickly fetched a fine new smooth-running mule-waggon and lashed a wicker basket on it. They took down from its peg a yoke of box-wood for the mules, with a knob in the middle and the proper guides for the reins; and with the yoke they brought out a yoke-binding four metres long. They laid the yoke carefully on to the polished shaft, in the notch at the front end of it, slipped the ring over the pin, tied the yoke-binding round the knob with three turns either way, then wound it closely round the shaft and tucked the loose end in under the hook.

This done, they went to the store-room, fetched the immense ransom that was to buy back Hector's body and packed it in the polished waggon. Then they yoked the sturdy mules who were trained to work in harness and had been a splendid gift to Priam from the Mysian people. Finally, they brought out Priam's chariot and yoked to it the horses that the old man kept for his own use and fed at the polished manger.

As Priam and the herald, with much to occupy their thoughts, organized the yoking of the mules and horses in the high palace, they were approached by Hecabe in great distress, carrying a golden cup of delicious wine in her right hand for them to make a drink-offering before they left. She came up to the chariot and spoke to Priam:

'Here, make a libation to Father Zeus and pray for your safe return from the enemy's hands, since you are set on going to the ships. You go against my will, but if go you must, address your prayer to Zeus son of Cronus who darkens the clouds, god of Mount Ida, who sees the whole region of Troy spread out beneath him. Ask for a bird of omen, a swift ambassador from him. And let it be his favourite prophetic bird, the strongest thing on wings, flying on your right so that you can see it with your own eyes and put your trust in it as you go down to the ships of the Greeks with their swift horses. But if far-thundering Zeus refuses to send you his messenger, I should advise you not to go down to the Greek ships, however much you may have set your heart on it.'

Godlike Priam replied and said:

'My dear, I will surely do as you suggest. It is a good thing to lift up one's hands to Zeus and ask him to have pity.'

The old man spoke and told his housekeeper to pour pure water over his hands. She brought a jug and basin and attended on him. When he had washed his hands, he took the cup from his wife, went to the middle of the forecourt to pray, looked up into the sky as he poured out the wine and said:

'Father Zeus, you that rule from Mount Ida, greatest and most glorious! Grant that Achilles receives me with kindness and mercy; and send me a bird of omen, your swift ambassador, your favourite prophetic bird, the strongest thing on wings, flying on my right, so I can see it with my own eyes and put my trust in it as I go down to the ships of the Greeks with their swift horses.'

So he spoke in prayer, and Zeus wise in counsel heard him and instantly sent out an eagle, the most perfect of prophetic birds, the dusky hunter they call the golden eagle, whose spread wings would span the width of a well-bolted door of the lofty chamber in a rich man's house. They saw it flying on their right across the town and were overjoyed at the sight. It warmed the hearts of everyone.

The old man quickly mounted his chariot and drove out

by the gateway and its echoing colonnade. He was preceded by the four-wheeled waggon, drawn by the mules and driven by wise Idaeus. Then came Priam's chariot. The old man used his whip and drove it quickly through the town; yet even so his whole family kept up with him, lamenting incessantly as though he were going to his death. But when they had made their way down through the streets and reached the plain, the people, his sons and sons-in-law, turned back into Ilium and went home.

Far-thundering Zeus saw the two men strike out across the plain. He felt pity for the old man and immediately said to his son Hermes:

'Hermes, escorting men is your greatest pleasure, and you listen to the requests of those you favour. So off you go now and conduct lord Priam to the Greeks' hollow ships in such a way that not a single Greek sees and recognizes him till he reaches Achilles.'

So he spoke, and the guide and slayer of Argus complied, and bound under his feet his lovely sandals, golden and imperishable, that carried him with the speed of the wind over the water and the boundless earth; and he picked up the wand which he can use at will to cast a spell on men's eyes or wake them from sleep. With this wand in his hand the mighty slayer of Argus made his flight and soon reached Troy and the Hellespont. There he proceeded on foot, looking like a young lord at that most charming age when the beard first starts to grow.

Meanwhile the two men had driven past the great grave-mound of Ilus and stopped their mules and horses for a drink at the river. Night was coming on by now.

When Hermes was quite close to them, the herald Idaeus looked up and saw him, and said to Priam:

'Look out, Priam. We must be very careful. I can see someone. I think we're going to be butchered. Quick, let's make our escape in the chariot, or if not that, fall at his knees and beg him for mercy.'

So he spoke, and the old man was completely bewildered and filled with terror; the hairs stood up on his bent limbs; he stood there, paralysed. But Hermes the runner went straight up to Priam, took him by the hand, questioned him and said:

'Father, where are you driving to with those horses and mules through the immortal night when everyone else is asleep? Aren't you afraid of the Greeks, breathing courage, those deadly enemies of yours, so close at hand? If any one of them saw you coming through the black night with such a valuable load, what could you do? You are not young enough to cope with anyone that might assault you; and your companion is an old man too. However, I certainly do not mean you harm. In fact, I am going to see that no one else molests you; for you remind me of my own father.'

The old man godlike Priam replied:

'Our plight, dear child, is very much as you describe. But even so some god must have extended a protecting hand over me when he let me fall in with a traveller like you, who come as a godsend, so distinguished are your looks and bearing, as well as your good sense. Your parents must be blessed.'

The guide and slayer of Argus replied:

'Sir, everything you have said is right. Now answer my questions and tell me exactly. Are you sending a splendid haul of treasure to some place of safety in a foreign land? Or has the time come when you are all deserting sacred Ilium in panic at the loss of your greatest warrior, your own son, who never let anyone down in battle against the enemy?'

The old man godlike Priam replied:

'Who are you, good sir? Who are your parents? How wonderfully you speak to me of the fate of my unhappy son.'

The guide and slayer of Argus replied:

'You're testing me, venerable sir, and trying to discover what I know about godlike Hector. Well, I have seen him with my own eyes – and seen him often – in battle where men win glory. And what's more, I saw him drive back the Greeks on to their own ships and mow them down with his sharp spear, while we Myrmidons stood by and marvelled, since Achilles would not let us fight, having quarrelled with lord Agamemnon.

'I am the attendant of Achilles and came here in the same good ship as he. I am a Myrmidon, and my father is Polyctor, a rich man and about as old as yourself. He has seven sons, of whom I am the youngest; and when we drew lots, it fell to me to join the expedition here. Tonight I left the ships and came out on to the plain because at daybreak the dark-eyed Greeks are intending to assault the town. They are tired of just sitting there and so eager for a fight that the Greek leaders cannot hold them back.'

The old man godlike Priam replied:

'If you really are an attendant of Peleus' son Achilles, come, tell me the whole truth: is my son still by the ships, or has Achilles already cut him up and thrown him piecemeal to his dogs?'

The guide and slayer of Argus replied:

'So far, venerable sir, neither the dogs nor birds of prey have eaten him. His body is intact and lies there in Achilles' hut beside his ship, just as it was. And though he has been there for eleven days, his flesh has not decayed at all nor has it been attacked by the worms that devour the bodies of men killed in battle. It is true that every day when bright Dawn appears Achilles drags him mercilessly round the grave-mound of his beloved companion; but that does not defile him. If you went into his hut yourself, you would be astonished to see him lying there as fresh as dew, the blood all washed away and not a mark on him. His wounds too have healed, every wound he had; and there were many men who stabbed him with their spears. This shows what care the blessed gods are taking of your son, dead though he is, because he was very dear to them.'

So he spoke, and the old man rejoiced and said:

'My child, what an excellent thing it is to give the gods their proper offerings! I am thinking of my son – if ever he was my son – and how he never neglected the gods of Olympus in our home. That is why they are repaying him like this, even though he has met his destiny and died. But here, accept this beautiful cup from me, keep me safe and, under the protecting hand of the gods, escort me till I reach Achilles' hut.'

The guide and slayer of Argus replied:

'You are an old man, sir, and I am young, and you are testing me. But you will not persuade me when you tell me to take a bribe behind Achilles' back. I fear and respect my master too deeply to defraud him: the consequences for myself might be severe. However, I am ready to serve you as escort all the way to my home in famous Thessaly in Greece and to assist you loyally on board ship or on foot. No one would attack you through underestimating your guard.'

Hermes the runner spoke and leapt into the chariot, seized the whip and reins in his hands and put fresh heart into the horses and mules. When they came to the ditch and the wall round the ships, they found the sentries just beginning to prepare a meal. But the guide and slayer of Argus put them all to sleep, unfastened the gates, thrust back the bars and ushered Priam in with his waggon-load of precious gifts.

They went on to the lofty hut of Peleus' son Achilles. The Myrmidons had built it for their master with planks of deal cut by themselves and roofed it over with a rough thatch of reeds gathered in the meadows. It stood in the large enclosure they made for their master surrounded by a close-set fence, and the gate was fastened by a single pine-wood bar. It took three men to drive this mighty bolt home and three to draw it back; three ordinary men, of course – Achilles could work it by himself. Now Hermes the runner opened it up for the old man, drove in with the splendid presents for swift-footed Achilles, dismounted from the chariot and said to Priam:

'Venerable sir, an immortal god has been accompanying you. I am Hermes and my father sent me as your escort. But I shall leave you now, as I do not intend to enter into Achilles' presence. It would be reprehensible for mortals to entertain an immortal god face to face in that way. But go inside yourself, clasp Achilles' knees and, as you supplicate him, invoke his father and his lovely-haired mother and his son, if you want your words to go straight to his heart.'

With these words Hermes went off to high Olympus. Priam leapt from his chariot to the ground and, leaving Idaeus there to look after the horses and mules, walked straight into the hut where Achilles dear to Zeus usually sat. He found him inside. Most of his men were sitting some way off, but two of them, the warrior Automedon and Alcimedon ally of the War-god, were waiting on him busily, as he had just finished eating and drinking and the table had not yet been removed. Great Priam came in unobserved by them, went up to Achilles, grasped his knees and kissed his hands, those terrible, man-slaying hands that had killed so many of his sons. As a thick cloud of delusion possesses a man who, after murdering someone in his own country, seeks refuge abroad in the home of a wealthy man, and the onlookers are astounded, so Achilles was astounded when he saw godlike Priam. The others were astounded too and exchanged glances.

Supplicating Achilles, Priam addressed him:

'Remember your own father, godlike Achilles, who is the same age as I am and on the threshold of miserable

143

old age. No doubt his neighbours are tormenting him and there is nobody to protect him from the harm and damage they cause. Yet, while he knows you are still alive, he can rejoice in spirit and look forward day by day to seeing his beloved son come back from Troy.

'But my life has been dogged by calamity. I had the best sons in the whole of this broad realm and now not one, not one I say, is left. There were fifty when the Greek army arrived. Nineteen of them were borne by one mother and the rest to other women in my palace. Most of them have fallen in action, and the only one I could still count on, the mainstay of Ilium and its inhabitants – you killed him a short while ago, fighting for his native land. Hector. It is to get him back from you that I have now come to the Greek ships, bringing an immense ransom with me.

'Achilles, respect the gods and have pity on me, remembering your own father. I am even more entitled to pity, since I have brought myself to do something no one else on earth has done – I have raised to my lips the hands of the man who killed my sons.'

With these words he awoke in Achilles a longing to weep for his own father. Taking the old man's hand, Achilles gently put him from him, and they were both overcome by their memories: Priam, huddled at Achilles' feet, wept aloud for man-slaying Hector, and Achilles wept for his father, and then again for Patroclus. The house was filled with the sounds of their lamentation. But when godlike Achilles had had enough of tears and the longing had ebbed from mind and body, he leapt at once from his chair and in compassion for the old man's grey head and grey beard took him by the arm and raised him. Then he spoke winged words:

'Unhappy man of sorrows, you have indeed suffered much. How could you bring yourself to come alone to the Greek ships into the presence of a man who had killed so many of your fine sons? You must have a heart of iron. Here now, be seated on this chair and, for all our grief, let us leave our sorrows locked up in our hearts, for weeping is cold comfort and does little good. We men are wretched creatures and the gods have woven grief into our lives: but they themselves are free from care.

'Zeus who delights in thunder has two jars standing on the floor of his palace in which he keeps his gifts, evils in one and blessings in the other. People who receive from him a mixture of the two enjoy varying fortunes, sometimes good and sometimes bad. But when Zeus serves a man from the jar of evil only, he debases him; ruinous hunger drives him over the bright earth and he goes his way respected by no one, god or man.

'Look at my father Peleus. From the moment he was born, the gods showered splendid gifts on him, fortune and wealth unparalleled among men, lordship over the Myrmidons and, though he was a man, a goddess for his wife. But the god also gave him his share of evil – no children in his palace to follow in his steps, only a single son and he destined for an untimely death. What is more, even though he is growing old, he gets no care from me because I am sitting around here in Troy far from the land of my fathers, seeing to you and your children.

'Now we have heard, venerable sir, there was a time when fortune smiled on you. They say there was no one to compare with you for wealth and sons in all the lands that are enclosed between Lesbos out to sea where Macar reigned, Phrygia inland and the vast Hellespont. But ever since the Sky-gods brought me here to be your scourge, there has been nothing but warfare and carnage round your city.

'Endure and do not mourn without end. Lamenting for your son will do no good at all. You will not bring him back to life before you are dead yourself.'

The old man godlike Priam replied:

'Do not ask me to sit down, Olympian-born Achilles, while Hector lies neglected in your huts, but give him back to me without delay and let me set my eyes on him. Accept the great ransom I bring. May you enjoy it and return safely to the land of your fathers, since from the very first you spared my life.'

Looking blackly at him swift-footed Achilles replied:

'Now don't push me too far, venerable sir. I have made my mind up without your help to give Hector back to you. A messenger from Zeus came to me – my very own mother that bore me, daughter of the Old Man of the Sea. What's more, I know all about you, Priam; you cannot hide the fact that some god brought you to the Greek ships. Nobody, not even a young man, would venture by himself into our camp. For one thing, he would never get past the sentries; and if he did, he would find it hard to shift the bar across the gate. So don't provoke my grief-stricken heart any more, sir, or I may break the commands of Zeus and, suppliant though you are in my huts, fail to spare your life.'

So he spoke, and the old man was afraid and did as he was told. Then, like a lion, Achilles leapt out of doors, taking with him two of his attendants, the warrior Automedon and Alcimedon, the men closest to him after the dead Patroclus. They unyoked the horses and the mules, brought in the herald, old Priam's crier, and sat him down. Then they took out of the polished waggon the immense ransom for Hector's body. But they left a couple of white mantles and a well-woven tunic in which Achilles could wrap the body when he gave it to Priam to take home.

Achilles then called out some waiting-women and told them to wash and anoint the body but in another part of his quarters, so that Priam should not see his son. Achilles was afraid that Priam, if he saw him, might in the bitterness of his grief be unable to control his anger; and then his own feelings would be provoked into killing the old man and breaking the commands of Zeus. When the waiting-women had washed and anointed the body with olive-oil and wrapped it in the fine mantle and tunic, Achilles lifted it with his own hands on to a bier, and his comrades helped him to put it in the well-polished waggon. Then he gave a groan and called on his dear companion by name:

'Patroclus, do not be indignant with me if you learn, down in the halls of Hades, that I let his father have god-like Hector back. The ransom he paid me was a worthy one and I will see that you receive your proper share of it.'

Godlike Achilles spoke and returned to his hut, sat down on the inlaid chair he had left – it was on the wall opposite Priam – and said:

'Your demands are granted, venerable sir: your son has been released. He is lying on the bier and at daybreak you will see him for yourself as you take him away. Now let us turn our thoughts to food.

'Even lovely-haired Niobe remembered to eat – and that was after she had seen her twelve children done to death in her own house, six daughters and six sons in their prime. Artemis who delights in arrows had killed the daughters; and Apollo with his silver bow shot down the sons. He was furious with Niobe for seeing herself as the equal of their own mother, lovely-cheeked Leto, and contrasting the many children she had produced with the two that Leto bore. Yet that pair, though they were only two, killed all of hers; and for nine days the children lay in pools of blood, as there was no one to bury them, Zeus son of Cronus having turned the people into stone. But on the tenth day the Sky-gods buried them, and Niobe, exhausted by her tears, made up her mind to take some food. And now, turned to stone, she stands among the crags in the lonely hills of Sipylus – where people say the Nymphs, when they have been dancing on the banks of River Achelous, lay themselves down to sleep. There Niobe broods on the desolation the gods dealt her.

'So now, venerable lord, let us two also think of food. Later, you can weep once more for your son, when you take him into Ilium. He will indeed be much mourned.'

Swift Achilles spoke, leapt up and slaughtered a white sheep which his men skinned and carefully prepared in the usual manner. They deftly chopped it up into small pieces, pierced the pieces on spits, roasted them carefully and then withdrew them from the fire. Automedon fetched some bread and set it out on the table in handsome baskets; Achilles divided the meat into portions; and they helped themselves to the good things spread before them.

Their hunger and thirst satisfied, Dardanian Priam let his eyes dwell on Achilles and saw with admiration how large and handsome he was, the very image of the gods. And Achilles dwelt with equal admiration on the noble looks and utterance of Dardanian Priam. When they had had their fill of gazing on each other, the old man godlike Priam spoke first:

'Send me to bed now, Olympian-bred Achilles, so that Idaeus and I can get our fill of sweet sleep. My eyelids have not closed over my eyes since the moment my son lost his life at your hands. Ever since then, I have been lamenting and brooding over my countless sorrows, grovelling in the dung in my stable-yard. Now at last I have tasted some food and poured sparkling wine down my throat; but before that I had tasted nothing.'

He spoke, and Achilles instructed his men and waiting-women to put beds in the portico and cover them with fine purple rugs, spread blankets over these and add some thick cloaks on top for covering. Torches in hand, the women left the room and set to work preparing the two beds. Now swift-footed Achilles spoke to Priam, causing him some agitation:

'Sleep out of doors, old friend, in case some Greek counsellor pays me a visit. They always come here to discuss tactics with me – it is our custom. If one of them were to see you here at dead of night, he would at once tell Agamemnon shepherd of the people, and your recovery of the body would be delayed. Now answer my question and tell me exactly how many days you propose to devote to godlike Hector's funeral, so that I myself refrain from fighting and ensure the army does too for that space of time.'

The old man godlike Priam replied:

'If you really wish me to give godlike Hector a proper funeral, you would do me a kindness, Achilles, by acting as follows. You know how we are cooped up in the town; it is a long journey to the mountains to fetch wood, and the Trojans are afraid of making it. We would be nine days mourning Hector in our homes. On the tenth we would bury him and hold the funeral feast, and on the eleventh build him a grave-mound. On the twelfth we will fight, if we really have to.'

Swift-footed godlike Achilles replied:

'Venerable Priam, everything shall be as you require. I will hold up the fighting for the time you have demanded.'

With these words he took the old man by the wrist of his right hand to banish all fear from his heart. So Priam and the herald settled down for the night there in the forecourt of the building, with much to occupy their thoughts. But Achilles slept in a corner of his well-made hut; and fair-cheeked Briseis slept beside him.

The other gods and fighting men slept through the night, conquered by soft sleep. But Hermes the runner kept wondering how he was going to bring lord Priam away from the ships without the guards noticing; and he could not get to sleep. So he went and stood over Priam's head and said:

'Venerable sir, since Achilles spared you, you seem to have no misgivings left, to judge by how soundly you sleep among your enemies. Just now you ransomed your son's body at a great price: your sons that are left would have to give three times as much to ransom you alive, if Agamemnon son of Atreus and the whole Greek army got to know you were here.'

So he spoke, and the old man was afraid and woke up his herald. Hermes then yoked the mules and horses for them and drove them quickly through the camp himself; they passed unrecognized. As saffron-robed Dawn spread over the world, they reached the ford of the sweetly flowing river, eddying Scamander whose father is immortal Zeus. There Hermes set out for high Olympus; and the two men, groaning and lamenting, drove the horses on towards the town while the mules came along with the body.

Cassandra, who looked like golden Aphrodite, was the first among the men and women of Troy to recognize them as they came. She had climbed to the top of Pergamus and from that point she saw her dear father standing in the chariot with the herald, his town-crier.

Then she saw him too, lying on the bier in the mule-waggon. She gave a scream and shouted aloud for all the town to hear:

'Trojans and women of Troy, if ever in the past you welcomed Hector back when he came home safe from battle – a moment for everyone in the town to rejoice – come out and see him now!'

So she spoke, and the whole town was plunged into inconsolable grief. Soon there was not a man or woman left in Ilium. They met Priam with Hector's body at no great distance from the gates. His dear wife and lady mother threw themselves on the smooth-running waggon, to be the first to tear their hair in mourning for him and touch his head. They were surrounded by a weeping throng. Indeed, they would have stayed there by the gates and wept for Hector all day long till sunset, if the old man had not spoken out from his chariot:

'Let me through with the mules. You can mourn for Hector to your hearts' content when I have got him home.'

So he spoke, and they fell back on either side and made a passage for the waggon. When the family had brought Hector into the palace, they laid him on an elaborate bed and set beside him dirge-singers to lead the laments and chant their melancholy songs, while the women took up the cry. White-armed Andromache, holding the head of man-slaying Hector between her hands, began her dirge:

'Husband, you were too young to die and leave me widowed in our home. Your son, the boy we luckless parents brought into the world, is but a little baby. And I have no hope that he will grow to manhood: Ilium will come tumbling to the ground before that can ever be. For you, her guardian, have perished, you that watched over her, you that kept her cherished wives and little babies safe. They will be carried off soon in the hollow ships, and I with them.

'And you, my child, will go with me to labour somewhere at degrading tasks under the eye of a merciless master; or some Greek will seize you by the arm and hurl you from the walls to an ugly death, venting his fury on you because Hector perhaps killed a brother of his, maybe, or else a father, or a son. Yes, at Hector's hands many a Greek bit the dust of the broad earth; for your father was no gentle soul in the cruelty of battle.

'And that is why everyone in Ilium now laments him. Ah, Hector, you have brought untold tears and misery to your parents. But my grief is cruellest of all, because you did not die reaching out from our bed to me with your arms, or utter some memorable word I might have treasured night and day through my tears.'

So she spoke in tears, and the women took up the cry. Hecabe now led the women in a shrill lament:

'Hector, dearest to me of all my sons, you were dear to the gods too while you were with me in the world; and even now you have met your destiny and died, it turns out they still care for you. Swift-footed Achilles took other sons of mine and sent them over the murmuring seas for sale in Samothrace or in Imbros or in misty Lemnos. And he took your life with his long spear; but though he dragged you many times round the gravemound of Patroclus, the companion of his you killed, that did not bring Patroclus back to life. But you have come home to me fresh as the dew and lie in the palace like one whom Apollo lord of the silver bow has visited and put to death with his gentle shafts.'

So she spoke in tears, and aroused unbridled grief. Helen then led them in a third lament:

'Hector, dearest to me of all my Trojan brothers, god-like Paris brought me here to Troy and married me – I wish I had perished first – but in all the nineteen years since I came away and left the land of my fathers, I never heard a single harsh or spiteful word from you. Others in the palace insulted me – your brothers, your sisters, your brothers' well-robed wives and your mother, though your father was the soul of kindness. But you calmed them down every time and stopped them out of the gentleness of your heart, with your gentle words. So these tears of sorrow I shed are both for you and for my luckless self. No one else is left in the wide realm of Troy to treat me kindly and befriend me. They all shudder at me.'

So she spoke in tears, and the vast multitude took up the cry. Now the old man Priam spoke to the people:

'Trojans, bring firewood to the town and do not be afraid of a Greek ambush. Achilles assured me, when he let me leave the black ships, that they would do us no harm till the dawn of the twelfth day from then.'

So he spoke, and they yoked mules and bullocks to their waggons and assembled speedily outside the town. Over nine days they gathered a huge supply of wood. When the dawn of the tenth day brought light to the world, they carried out daring Hector, weeping, laid his body on top of the pyre and lit it.

But when early-born, rosy-fingered Dawn appeared, the people flocked together round glorious Hector's pyre. When everyone had assembled and the gathering was complete, they first put out with sparkling wine whatever was still burning. Then Hector's brothers and comrades-in-arms collected his white bones, lamenting and with many a tear running down their cheeks. They took the bones, wrapped them in soft purple clothing and put them in the golden coffin. This coffin they immediately lowered into a hollow grave which they covered with a close-set layer of large stones. They hurriedly piled up earth over it to mark the grave-mound, posting guards all round in case the Greeks launched a premature attack. When they had piled up the mound, they returned into the city and reassembled for a magnificent funeral feast in the palace of Priam their Olympian-bred ruler.

Such were the funeral rites of horse-taming Hector.